Just a show. That was the key.

Except it wasn't.

Yes, the only reason his first kiss with his wife was taking place in front of a captive audience was to prove a point—to show them that Helena wasn't some sort of poor consolation prize. But that wasn't enough. He had to show Helena that, too.

And Helena knew the truth.

If he wanted her to stick with this, to believe they had a real future together, well...that future started right now. With their first kiss.

"Kiss, kiss, kiss, kiss!" The chanting around them faded into nothing as he leaned in closer, his eyes closing as his lips brushed against hers, soft at first, not wanting to spook her. But then, God, then... Flynn's fingers clutched at her hip, the silk of her dress slipping against his skin as he deepened the kiss.

She tasted like champagne and gold, expensive and sparkling, her mouth warm and willing under his.

He'd wanted to p   point with this kiss, but for the life of him   member what it was.

Dear Reader,

When I finished writing Thea and Zeke's story in *A Groom Worth Waiting For*, I knew I couldn't stop there. Helena and Flynn were still stuck in that Tuscan villa, with two hundred plus of their fathers' nearest and dearest business associates, plus the media, all waiting for the wedding of the year.

I had to know what they'd do next.

The story that followed is one of my favorites that I've written so far. I loved the challenge of *starting* with a wedding, rather than ending with one. And I already knew from the first book that Helena and Flynn had some rather dramatic differences of opinion, history and experience that would make any romance between them tempestuous—but incredibly worthwhile.

So, from a luxury villa in Italy, through vineyards and jewelry shops, and back to the rainy streets of London, I hope you enjoy following Helena and Flynn as they travel toward their happy-ever-after. Even if it turns out that what they thought would make them happy isn't what they need at all...

Love and confetti,

Sophie

His Very Convenient Bride

Sophie Pembroke

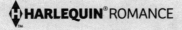

HARLEQUIN® ROMANCE

Recycling programs
for this product may
not exist in your area.

ISBN-13: 978-0-373-74321-6

His Very Convenient Bride

First North American Publication 2015

Copyright © 2015 by Sophie Pembroke

Printed in U.S.A.

Sophie Pembroke has been dreaming, reading and writing romance for years—ever since she first read *The Far Pavilions* under her desk in chemistry class. She later stayed up all night devouring Harlequin books as part of her English degree at Lancaster University and promptly gave up any pretext of enjoying tragic novels. After all, what's the point of a book without a happy ending?

She loves to set her novels in the places where she has lived—from the wilds of the Welsh mountains to the genteel humor of an English country village or the heat and tension of a London summer. She also has a tendency to make her characters kiss in castles.

Currently Sophie makes her home in Hertfordshire, UK, with her scientist husband (who still shakes his head at the reading-in-chemistry thing) and their four-year-old *Alice in Wonderland*–obsessed daughter. She writes her love stories in the study she begrudgingly shares with her husband while drinking too much tea and eating homemade cakes. Or, when things are looking very bad for her heroes and heroines, white wine and dark chocolate.

Sophie keeps a blog at sophiepembroke.com, which should be about romance and writing but is usually about cake and castles instead.

Books by Sophie Pembroke

HARLEQUIN ROMANCE

A Groom Worth Waiting For
Heiress on the Run
Stranded with the Tycoon

Visit the Author Profile page at Harlequin.com for more titles

For Pippa, for everything.

CHAPTER ONE

FLYNN STARED AT HER, a hint of panic in his usually calm and collected brown eyes. Helena gazed back, hoping she looked slightly less like a small wild animal caught in the open by a predator than he did.

She had to admit, though, that was unlikely. This was very new territory for both of them.

'While I know that what we just did was very noble and right and championed the cause of true love and so on…what on earth do we do now?' Flynn asked.

Helena's mind whirred with the possibilities, just as it had been doing since the moment her sister ran out of the door, leaving her holding both the pearl-encrusted ivory wedding dress and the proverbial baby. They didn't have much in the way of options, and one choice kept rising to the top of the very short list.

'Help me out of this dress.' She placed Thea's wedding dress carefully on a padded armchair, then twisted to try and reach the zip at the back of her own flamingo-pink bridesmaid's dress. Not a chance. No one had arms that bent like that.

She looked up at Flynn. He was still staring at her.

Men. Hopeless in a crisis.

Although, actually, before today she'd have wagered that Flynn would be pretty good in an emergency. By all accounts, he'd handled the discovery that his fiancée had slept with his brother less than twenty-four hours before their wedding with remarkable aplomb. He'd managed the news that he was about to inherit sole responsibility for a multinational media conglomerate without breaking a sweat. He'd even let the aforementioned fiancée, Helena's sister, run out and elope with her true love moments before the wedding without looking particularly perturbed.

But apparently Helena in her underwear was pushing him too far.

With a sigh, she turned to present him with her back and the offending zip. 'Just undo me, yeah?'

Flynn hesitated a moment before she felt his warm fingertips against her back. 'Why am I doing this?'

'Because I need to get changed. Into that.' She pointed at the wedding dress and felt Flynn's hands still at her back.

'No. No, you don't. We'll just go down to the church and…'

She spun round to face him. 'And what? Tell every business associate you have plus a nice collection of reporters—not to mention both sets of parents—that the wedding of the year is off?' Helena shook her head. That option was very firmly a last resort. Never mind the tabloid fallout, or the impact on company shares—her father would have a heart attack.

'Surely that has to be better than us getting...' He waved a hand between them and she rolled her eyes.

'Married, Flynn. Go on, you can say it. It's not actually a dirty word. You were all set to do it with my sister, and I suspect you weren't any more in love with her than she was with you. As evidenced by the fact you just told her to elope with Zeke.'

'That was different,' Flynn argued. 'Thea and I had a plan. There was...paperwork.'

The man was completely business bound. Grabbing the file the wedding planner had put together for Thea, Helena pulled out a spare invitation, grabbed the pen from its loop and scratched out her sister's name to replace it with her own. Then, as an afterthought, she scribbled a few lines on the back on it. 'Paperwork,' she said, handing it to Flynn. 'Happy now?'

'"I, Helena Morrison, promise to marry Flynn Ashton purely to avoid the hideous fallout of my sister's elopement,"' Flynn read. 'Helena, this is—'

'Keep going.' Helena reached behind her to try and work the zip down the last few inches, finally succeeding in wriggling the strapless dress past her hips and into a heap on the floor.

Flynn turned his back on her, and Helena bit back a smile. He was so *proper*.

'"Furthermore, I agree to renegotiate this contract once the official Morrison-Ashton company business issue thing is dealt with. Signed, Helena Morrison."' He placed the makeshift contract carefully on the table as if it were a real and important document. 'Company business issue thing?' he asked, sounding puzzled.

'You know—the whole reason you and Thea were supposed to be getting married in the first place. Whatever that was.' Helena stepped into her sister's wedding dress and prayed to God that it fitted well enough to avoid comment. Thea was taller by a couple of inches and Helena had more in the way of curves, but as long as it did up and she could avoid tripping over the hem she'd probably be okay.

'To join both sides of the business and provide…well, to give the company an heir.'

An heir. A child. Maybe even children, plural. Helena swallowed, then pulled the wedding dress up over her chest. She'd cross that very high and scary bridge when she got to it. Or not. Maybe she could dig a tunnel instead…

Okay, thinking was clearly not her friend today. The exhilaration of Thea's escape, of being the one left behind to fix things, of this whole crazy plan, thrummed through her veins. She felt high on excitement in a way she hadn't since she was sixteen.

What she was about to do might be insane but at least it made her feel *alive*.

For now, at least. 'This doesn't have to be a permanent arrangement, anyway,' she said, manoeuvring herself around to Flynn's side, wedding dress still trailing. 'Lace me up?' No zips for the bride. Apparently corset ties were the order of the day.

He obliged without argument, yanking the ties more than tight enough to keep the dress up and tying them in a very efficient bow at the base of her spine. Apparently she was about to marry the one straight man in Europe more comfortable with putting clothes on a woman than taking them off.

'That wasn't the arrangement with Thea,' he told her.

Helena spun round to face him, a fake smile on her face. 'Yes, well. I'm not Thea, am I?' Something she seemed to have been pointing out to disappointed friends, relatives and acquaintances for most of her life. Mostly her father, first wondering why she couldn't be better behaved, more obedient, less trouble. Until trouble had caught up with her at last and suddenly she was perfectly happy to stay home, stay out of trouble, stay safe.

But it hadn't been enough. Then he'd wanted to know why she couldn't have her sister's drive, or brains, or brilliance. Never mind that she *was* less trouble than Thea at last, that she kept their whole family on an even keel, dealing with the fallout from Thea's latest romantic mishaps.

Just like today, really.

This. This one thing—marrying her own sister's fiancé to safeguard the family name, business and reputation—if this didn't make up for the mistakes of her past, nothing ever would. This was her chance.

She could be enough for Flynn. She might not be Thea, but she was still a Morrison. She could give him what he needed, and maybe marrying him could give her absolution after eight long years in the wilderness.

As long as he never found out why she needed absolution. Flynn, of all people, would never understand that.

Flynn's eyes were serious as she looked into them, steady and firm, and Helena's smile slipped away. He was the ultimate man with the plan, she remembered from overheard business talk and the endless wedding preparations. Could he even do this? Be spontaneous enough to marry a stand-in bride?

'Are you sure you want to do this?' he asked, and Helena rolled her eyes.

'I don't think either of us can be sure about that, given that we've had all of about five minutes to think about it.' There was always a chance that she'd regret this moment, this idea for the rest of her life. But right then…the risk seemed worth it.

'I will walk down there and tell everyone it's off,' Flynn said. 'Just say the word, and you're free.'

Somehow, Helena knew that he'd planned to say those words anyway. That he'd have given Thea a last-minute out too, even if Zeke hadn't come home for the wedding. Flynn was a fair, kind, considerate man. And he might not have been the husband she'd imagined for herself, not least because he was supposed to have been her brother-in-law, but she could have done a lot worse. He was a safe choice. He'd never force her, or trick her or be anything but upfront and honest. It was…refreshing.

This could work, one way or another. Maybe they could make a friendly marriage, for the sake of the family and the business. Or, more likely, it might last a month and then they'd quietly end the whole thing. Either was fine. Flynn wouldn't make a fuss; she knew that much about him. They were the calm two now, the ones who smoothed over rough edges at social gatherings, who kept the joint family dinners his mother insisted on civil, even in the face of insurmountable odds. Between them they'd even hidden the fact that Thea and Zeke had slept together on the villa terrace *during the rehearsal dinner* from the hundred guests inside. Maybe they were meant to be together.

And even if it didn't last, the marriage would have served its purpose as a spectacular PR stunt for Morrison-Ashton and Flynn would be free to find a bride who'd give him heirs by the dozen, if he wanted. Win-win, really.

'I'm sure,' she said, and Flynn smiled.

'Then let's go to church.'

Flynn wasn't his brother. He didn't like surprises, didn't want the risk-taking high, or the buzz from making spur-of-the-moment decisions that Zeke seemed to crave. Flynn liked to work from a plan, to know what was coming and prepare accordingly. His very existence, and the fact of his birth, was the definition of unplanned—but Flynn had always felt that there was no reason his life had to follow the same pattern.

A childhood of believing he was an 'unexpected variable', or just a straightforward 'mistake'—depending on whether he was eavesdropping on his father or mother's conversation at the time—had made it very clear to him how deviating from a plan could screw things up. Never mind that *he'd* been the plan. It was Zeke who had come along and screwed everything up. But Zeke was blood, the true heir they'd really wanted but thought they couldn't have. Not somebody else's unwanted child, brought in to fill a void as a last resort.

If his parents had stuck with the plan and never had Zeke, Flynn's life could have been very, very different.

So Flynn prized structure, deliverables, timescales and, above all, a plan. But today, his *wedding day*, didn't appear to be about what Flynn liked or wanted.

He'd heard that before, from married friends. How the wedding day became all about the bride and her mother and her friends, and all the groom really had to do was show up and say 'I do'. Of course, every single one of those friends had actually married the woman they got engaged to...

Fear had clenched in his chest as Thea ran out of the door, tearing his carefully worked plan to shreds. Three years he'd been planning this, talking with his father, and hers, making sure they used the wedding to its full potential. Two years working on Thea, agreeing terms, gentling her along.

In the end, all the planning in the world hadn't been enough. Thea was gone, and that left him with…Helena.

Helena wasn't part of the plan, not even a little bit. She was another unplanned variable, he supposed. But maybe that meant something. Maybe together they could be more than a list of mistakes, of unexpected consequences.

Either way, she was the closest he was going to get to following his plan for the day.

He couldn't hide the relief he felt when he realised that Helena really planned to go through with her proposal. Yes, marrying his fiancée's sister raised its own collection of problems. And, yes, an argument could be made that any family or business situation that required this level of absurd subterfuge was seriously screwed up. And yet Flynn found himself agreeing that it was the best of a short list of bad options. Maybe it wasn't the original strategy, but it could at least be considered a contingency plan. It wasn't as if he hadn't discussed the possibility with his father, before settling on Thea as the most beneficial to the company.

This wasn't a love match and it never had been. Whichever of the Morrison sisters walked down the aisle on his arm, the purpose was served.

Thea might have understood a little better what she was letting herself in for, but Helena wasn't completely ignorant of the situation either.

Morrison-Ashton needed this. Its board, investors—everyone—needed to know that the future of the company was in safe hands.

And hands didn't come safer than Flynn Ashton's.

Flynn had his own reasons for wanting the match, of course, but surely Helena would realise that too. Thea had, quickly enough.

The company needed the PR boost and, even before he'd really believed he might inherit it one day, Morrison-Ashton had always been Flynn's priority. Now he stood to be CEO within the year…and he needed this more than ever. He needed the authenticity the match gave him. Married to one of the Morrison sisters, it wouldn't matter that he wasn't true Ashton blood. His adoption ceased to matter. Even the fact that his adoption had come through just as Ezekiel and Isabella Ashton had discovered that they were expecting their own flesh and blood child, Zeke, lost meaning as anything more than a crippling irony.

As a child, he'd been surplus to requirements, an inconvenience once the Ashtons had what they'd really wanted all along. And, as he'd grown older, he'd been a weapon in his father's hand, used to whip Zeke into shape, to make him earn his inheritance by fighting Flynn for every advantage, every opportunity. But as the husband of Thea—or Helena—Morrison, Flynn would be legitimate. Deserving.

He'd belong at last.

Taking Helena's hand, he led her out of Thea's dressing room, down the stairs and out of the front door into the blazing Tuscan sunshine. With her body close against his, he could feel the tension in its lines and wondered how fast her heart must be beating right now. Maybe even as hard and fast as his.

Because, despite all his rational thoughts, Flynn couldn't quite lie to himself well enough to pretend there wasn't a chance this would prove to be a colossal mistake. *This doesn't have to be a permanent arrangement.* Helena's words echoed around his head. To her, this was only temporary; she was a stand-in bride for the occasion. But temporary didn't fulfil Flynn's needs for this marriage.

He needed permanence, he needed authenticity and he needed heirs. That was the plan and, given everything else that had gone wrong, he had to cling on to those facts. Once he married Helena, she was his for life.

He'd just have to figure out a way to convince her that he could be enough for her, that he was worth staying for. Once they got through this horrendous, confusing day.

Flynn blinked in the sunlight. Everything felt somehow more real outside. The summer sounds on the breeze—insects and dry leaves—disappeared behind a peal of bells from the chapel below.

This was really happening. Maybe not the way he'd planned, but the outcome would be more or less the same. He would have made it at last, the moment Helena said 'I do'. And she would, he was sure. She'd been so fierce, so determined to make this work. Why? he wondered suddenly. What did it matter to her? Or was she just so afraid of their parents' wrath that she'd do anything to appease them?

Maybe he'd ask her. Afterwards.

They walked down the path to the chapel in silence, as quickly as Helena's heels would allow. Flynn glanced down at her feet, catching glimpses of the flamingo-pink satin heels that would have matched her bridesmaid's dress. Thea must have run out in her shoes.

Helena's gaze flicked down and she gave him a rueful smile. 'She took the veil, too. Shame, really. We could have kept my face hidden until it was all over, otherwise.'

Something caught in Flynn's chest. Maybe his wedding to Thea hadn't been a grand epic romance but it had been better than this. Helena deserved better than this.

'I don't want to hide you,' he said, hoping it was enough. 'You're going to be my wife. And I'm proud to have you at my side.' All true, even if he was more proud of her name than her person, for now. But Helena had been a sweet child and, since they'd started the wedding planning, a helpful, cheerful woman. Flynn had no doubt that in time he'd grow even fonder of her. Perhaps they'd even fall in love, if they were very lucky. As he'd hoped to do with Thea.

Helena's smile was a little sad but there was no more time to talk. As they rounded the corner to the chapel Thomas Morrison came into view, waiting to walk his daughter down the aisle.

'Helena! Where on earth is Thea? The mob is getting restless in there...' He stopped, staring at her as he took in the dress.

Flynn stepped forward, ready to jump the first hurdle for the pair of them. 'I'm afraid, sir, there's been a slight change of plan...'

As the string quartet struck up a new tune, Helena realised that, at the back of her mind, she'd expected her father to call their bluff. To tell them the whole idea was ridiculous and send everyone home. At the very least, she'd thought he'd have put up some sort of argument for reason.

But apparently it didn't much matter to him which of his daughters Flynn Ashton married, as long as he married one of them. Today.

The revelation stung a little more than she'd imagined it would after so many years of not being good enough.

This time, *please, this time,* she was going to be good enough.

'That's our cue,' her father whispered in her ear as the violins picked up the melody.

Helena nodded, focusing on not gripping her father's arm too hard as the church doors swung open.

She was really doing this. Marrying Flynn Ashton. And there was no parent or spurned lover about to run in and yell: *Stop the wedding!* Nobody to tell her she was making a colossal mistake, if she was. How could she tell, anyway? This wedding would get them through today and, right now, that was all that mattered. After that… well, she'd figure out what happened next once all these people had gone home.

It had been too much to hope that people might not notice that Flynn was marrying the wrong sister. From the moment the doors opened and Helena took her first step on to the tiled floor of the aisle, there were whispers. They ran through the pews like a wave, the cool and shady chapel suddenly buzzing with scandal and gossip. Helena couldn't make out the words but she could guess the sentiment.

What's happened? What's gone wrong? How did he end up with her? *What does this mean...?*

There were going to be a lot of questions over the next few hours, days and weeks, Helena realised. They'd got off lightly with her dad because there simply wasn't the time. People were waiting, and Thomas Morrison would not disappoint them. *You came to see my daughter get married? Well, here you go. What do you mean, it's the wrong one?*

Helena tried to suppress a giggle at the thought of her father trying to convince his guests that this marriage was what he'd intended all along, but a small squeak escaped. Her father's hand tightened on her arm and, when she glanced up at him, his expression was grim.

Suddenly, nothing was funny any more. Helena tried to focus on the posies of white flowers tied with satin ribbons at the end of each pew, or the pedestal displays—anything except the truth she saw in her father's face.

She'd thought that this would be enough, that marrying Flynn would make up for the past. But her father's expression told another story. If it didn't matter to him which of his daughters got married today, it didn't mean a thing.

Her slate would never be wiped clean, no matter what she did or how far she went. If eight years of being a perfect daughter hadn't been enough, why on earth had she imagined that marrying Flynn might do it? Thomas Morrison held grudges, and he held on tight. The best she could hope for was that Thea would be in so much trouble that she might eclipse Helena's own mistakes for a while.

Thea. How was she ever going to explain this to Thea?

Thea would have stopped her. But Thea was off chasing her own happy ever after, and Helena had stepped right into the very shoes she'd tried to talk her sister out of just a few days before.

Helena glanced down and caught a glimpse of her bright pink bridesmaid's shoes. Not quite Thea's white satin heels, after all. And this wedding, and everything that would follow, wasn't quite as it would have been for Thea, either. There was less paperwork, for a start. Just a scribbled unofficial contract at complete odds with the thirty-page document that had comprised Thea and Flynn's prenuptial agreement.

But, more than that, Helena wasn't Thea. She wasn't the face of the business and she was neither qualified nor willing to take on her sister's role at the company, presuming that Thea didn't come home to take it back herself. She was still a

Morrison, and maybe that was enough for Flynn and his father.

For the first time since she'd entered the church, Helena looked past the flowers, the hats and the gossips and stared at her husband-to-be. Standing there beside the priest, his feet slightly apart, hands behind his back, Flynn looked solid. Calm, reliable, steady. All the things Helena had never thought she wanted in her life until eight years ago. Things she'd thought she'd never be able to find, since.

A casual observer, watching his serene expression, would never guess that the woman he was marrying today wasn't the woman he'd proposed to.

Maybe Helena could earn some of that serenity for herself, by marrying Flynn. If she could be what he needed, then surely he could be enough for her. She just couldn't help but wonder how much he was going to ask of her, before she reached that magical point of *enough*.

Give the company an heir.

Terrifying words—words that sent a shudder through her whole body. But they were just words, part of Flynn's agreement with Thea. Not with her. Never her. Because he couldn't know, wouldn't understand—and so she couldn't tell him what a baby would mean to her. How it might destroy her, this time, just to think about it.

The past only stayed in the past until it got dragged into the present. Hadn't Thea and Zeke proved that?

Too late to question what she was doing now, anyway. He'd given her an out and she hadn't taken it. To run at this point would be worse than if she'd never suggested this stupid idea in the first place. No one would ever forgive her for humiliating Flynn Ashton on his wedding day—for letting it happen twice.

No, she was getting married today and all she could do now was make the most of it, until enough time had passed for a discreet divorce.

Head held high, Helena continued to stare down the aisle at her intended husband until suddenly he looked up and met her gaze. His eyes were steady and serious, just like the man himself. Flynn Ashton was stable, reliable—everything Helena needed in her life. He wouldn't let her screw up again; she knew it.

They reached the front row of seats and Flynn stepped forward to meet them for the ceremonial giving away of the bride. As she disentangled her hand from her father's arm, he leant in towards Flynn. 'She's your problem now, son,' he muttered, and Helena's heart stung.

No, even this wasn't enough for him to forgive her. She couldn't imagine why she'd ever thought it would be. That all of this could be anything except a huge mistake.

'I like to think she'll be my partner rather than my problem,' Flynn murmured back, and Helena's gaze flew to his face in surprise.

Maybe, just maybe, marrying Flynn wasn't a mistake. Maybe it was an opportunity.

Maybe it could even be her future.

With a bright smile, Helena turned, gave her father a dry peck on the cheek, then stepped forward in bright pink shoes to meet it.

CHAPTER TWO

HELENA'S HAND FELT warm in his, an unexpected heat in the cool shade of the chapel. There wasn't a lot of warmth coming from the congregation either. More frosty confusion and comments as sharp as icicles. Flynn squared his shoulders as they took the last couple of steps up to the altar together. He'd known this wouldn't be an easy sell but if there was one thing he'd learnt growing up as the cuckoo in the Ashton nest, it was how to smooth over ruffled feathers.

It was a talent that had served him well in business, too. He was the one they brought in when Ezekiel Ashton had offended an investor or a client. The one who talked secretaries into staying when they'd had the sharp edge of Zeke Senior's tongue one too many times.

But, more than that, he was the one who made things happen. Not by making threats, as Ezekiel did, or taking risks and dares as Zeke would have done, but by gentling people along until they almost thought whatever Flynn wanted was their own idea.

The same way he'd persuaded Thea to marry him, in fact.

But *Helena* was the plan now. He just had to smooth the way forward for them. Make it so that everyone realised that, while this particular wedding was unexpected, it was just what they'd all really wanted all along, even if they hadn't known it.

He'd made a good start at that, he hoped, with his comment to Thomas. After all, Thomas might own half the business but he'd leave it to Helena in the end, once she was married to him. He might even disown Thea altogether after today, not that it made much difference. Zeke had made it clear that he was never coming back to Morrison-Ashton. Flynn would be CEO within the year and he'd have Helena at his side.

Which meant Helena, not Thomas, was the important one now.

Another talent Flynn had learnt young: identify the vital person and focus on them. In a family argument, the vital person varied. Usually it was Ezekiel because he was the head of the household, the ultimate authority. Sometimes it was Isabella because her own power, especially over Ezekiel, couldn't be ignored. Occasionally it was Zeke, but only when two brothers teaming up together could win their parents round to their way of thinking, which wasn't often.

It went without saying that Flynn was never that vital person.

But he wasn't a mistake or an accident, not any more. Not an unfortunate addition or a spare part, to be dragged out when he could be useful. *He* was what the company needed. What the family needed. And all he needed was Helena.

He squeezed Helena's hand, just a small measure of reassurance as the priest smiled at them. Had the old man not realised that there was something amiss today? It was possible. Thea had been out the one time he'd come to call on them. The priest had spoken to Flynn and Helena instead, and had nodded amiably when Flynn had leant forward to murmur their names to him again before Helena walked down the aisle, just to make sure he got it right in the service. It was entirely possible that the man holding the Bible firmly believed that he was joining a young couple in love in the binding act of marriage.

Well, Flynn was on board with the binding part, at least.

As they knelt before the priest, he heard a gasp go up from the congregation behind them. Frowning, he glanced over at his bride and saw her trying to hide a smile behind her hand.

'What?' he mouthed, raising an eyebrow.

Helena gave a tiny shake of her head, but lowered her hand long enough to whisper, 'I think they just clocked the shoes.'

Of course. Those ridiculous pink shoes.

Flynn kept his eyes on the floor in front of him. In all honesty, he quite liked the shoes. Liked the flash of colour and spirit they showed, just like the woman wearing them had when she'd stepped into that wedding dress at the last moment. They were right for Helena.

But they weren't appropriate for a Morrison-Ashton bride, of course. Not for a formal, prestigious event like this. Especially when they were on the wrong feet.

He couldn't let those pink high heels ruin everything. Everything else could go perfectly, Helena could be a perfect blushing bride, and all it would take would be the wrong society matron friend of his mother's saying, 'But did you see those *shoes?*' and suddenly everyone would have permission to pick the whole marriage apart.

As if they weren't going to do that anyway.

Flynn sighed, resigned himself to making the best of a bad day and tried to tune in to what the priest was saying. Before he knew it, they were at the only part of the service that really mattered—the promises and vows.

'Flynn and Helena, have you come here freely and without reservation to give yourself to each other in marriage?' The priest intoned the words with the sort of gravity that made it clear these were serious questions.

Flynn exchanged a fleeting glance with Helena as they both answered, 'Yes.' He wondered if she was thinking the same thing that he was—that he had many, many reservations about this. But he was going to go through with it anyway.

'Will you honour each other as man and wife for the rest of your lives?'

'I will,' Flynn said, Helena's agreement coming just a heartbeat behind.

She'd said it now, and that knowledge filled Flynn with triumph. The rest of their lives. That was exactly how long he needed to prove he deserved this—his place in the family and the business. He knew the board members and the investors. He knew what they needed in order to believe in and respect Flynn's new place at Morrison-Ashton.

Ezekiel Ashton had made it clear for years that Flynn didn't count, that he wasn't a true heir. Even if Zeke hadn't known it, everyone else associated with the business had never doubted for a moment that Zeke was the one who'd inherit.

But not any more. Now that place was Flynn's and the next few moments would cement it for life.

'Will you accept children lovingly from God,

and bring them up according to the law of Christ and his Church?'

Beside him, Helena sucked in a breath, just loud enough for him to hear. As if she was steeling herself for something unpleasant. He frowned.

'I will,' Helena said, strong and clear, but Flynn couldn't shake the feeling that he'd just missed something important.

Like saying his line.

'I will,' he said, aware of the priest's waiting gaze.

'Good.' The priest cracked a creaky smile. 'Then, next, we have the vows. Flynn?'

He'd memorised this, had been prepared to stare into Thea's eyes and say just the right words. But now, as he turned to face his bride and take her hand, looking down further than he'd expected to, Flynn realised he hadn't a clue what her middle name was.

His panic must have shown on his face because Helena rolled her eyes and mouthed 'Juliette' at him, allowing his heartbeat to return to normal again.

'I, Flynn, take you, Helena Juliette Morrison, to be my wife.' She smiled as he spoke, and Flynn relaxed into the familiar words. 'I promise to be true to you in good times and in bad, in sickness and in health. I will love you and honour you, all the days of my life.'

He hoped she could hear how much he meant it. Love…maybe that would come and maybe it wouldn't. But honour, constancy and fidelity—those he could give her.

It was the least he could do, given what he would gain from the bargain. She was his now, along with the respectability and the place she brought him. It was done at last.

Flynn couldn't help but think he should feel more relieved about that.

'I, Helena, take you, Flynn Michael Ashton, to be my husband.' The words came out strong and clear, and Helena gave silent thanks that the trembling taking over her insides wasn't visible or audible to the congregation. She'd learnt the vows by heart practising them with Thea; she could recite them with her eyes closed. Which might actually be easier than staring up into Flynn's face, trying to look suitably besotted and loving.

Every single person listening was waiting to see if they'd really go through with it. Maybe some thought it was a stunt, some crazy PR thing. Maybe they even believed that Thea would appear from the wings to take her rightful place at any moment.

Wow. Those people were going to be *really* disappointed.

Most people, Helena suspected, were just waiting to see if this marriage would really happen, and hoping that at some point over the next few hours they'd find out why.

This was the scandal of the year, and not one of Isabella's friends would rest until they knew what had really happened behind the scenes today.

Isabella. Helena sneaked a sideways look at the front pew as she promised to be true, to love and honour and all the rest of that stuff. Flynn and Zeke's mother sat with a fixed smile on her face, hands clasped around a handkerchief in her lap, the wide brim of her hat shading her eyes. Helena would bet that if she could see any tears in them, they wouldn't be tears of joy.

Explaining this mess to Flynn's parents was not going to be fun. Maybe she'd leave that to him. Refine the art of wifely delegating early.

Her vows done, the priest picked up the baton again. 'What God has joined, man must not divide,' he intoned.

Gosh, that sounded formal. Binding.

Final.

Well, what did he know? He'd happily married the wrong couple without batting an eyelid. There was a pretty strong chance that none of this was even legal. It would be fine.

'Do you have the rings?' the priest asked, and Helena's eyes widened. Did they? What had even happened to them?

But Flynn reached into his jacket pocket and pulled out a ring box, flipping open the lid to reveal two shiny platinum rings. Helena knew those rings, had helped choose those rings.

She also knew there was a good chance that the ring Flynn was about to try and put on her finger wouldn't fit.

As the priest blessed the rings, Helena tried to convey this information to her new husband using only her eyes and eyebrows. Anything else would signal to their audience that there was a problem.

Flynn's forehead furrowed in confusion and Helena resigned herself to losing the outer layer of skin on her ring finger.

'Helena, take this ring as a sign of my love and fidelity.' Flynn took her left hand solemnly and Helena braced herself as the cold metal touched the tip of her finger. 'In the name of the Father, and of the Son and of the Holy Spirit.'

Flynn eased the ring down to her knuckle, where it promptly got stuck. His gaze flashed to hers and she gave him what she hoped was an imperceptible shake of the head.

He understood, thank goodness. His fingers moved down to the base of her finger, but the ring stayed jammed where it was. With a sunny smile, Helena withdrew her hand and hid it in the folds of her dress. She'd ease it further on later, if she could. Otherwise she'd sneak up to her room and find some other ring to serve for the time being.

Flynn's ring slipped on with no problems, of course, since he was actually supposed to be there getting married today. And suddenly the priest was pronouncing them husband and wife and it was all over. Helena blinked out at the applauding crowd and felt grateful that the line 'You may now kiss the bride' seemed to appear more often in movies than at actual weddings.

She was married now. And she did realise that the chances were she'd have to kiss her husband, sooner or later.

It was just that she was voting for later. When her emotions and thoughts weren't spinning like a tornado. When she could sit quietly for a moment and figure all this out, and think about what would happen next.

When she'd had time to prepare herself.

With her hand tucked into the crook of Flynn's elbow, hiding the ill-fitting wedding ring, Helena walked back up the aisle she'd walked down as a single woman. As Helena Morrison.

Now she was Helena Ashton.

She was pretty sure she would never get used to that.

Helena fought to keep her expression bright and happy, tilting her head to brush against Flynn's shoulder as they walked.

'Nearly there,' he murmured as they approached the back of the church. 'Almost over.'

Except it wasn't. Not even a little bit.

The Tuscan sunlight stung her eyes and her skin as they emerged from the cool shade of the chapel. They only had a few moments before everyone else followed, so Helena ripped her hand from Flynn's arm and began to twist Thea's wedding ring over her knuckle. If only she had some hand cream in her bag. Or even her bag.

Brides travelled light, it seemed.

With a pop, the ring slid past the knuckle and into place, and Helena exhaled with relief. One problem down, who knew how many more to go.

As the guests emerged, Helena plastered her best social smile back on to her face. Which, as the first person out was Ezekiel Ashton, was a bit of a waste.

'What, exactly—?' the old man started, only to be cut off by his wife.

'Not here,' Isabella said, her voice quiet but sharp. Helena had no doubt that there would be long discussions about what had occurred that day, but Isabella wouldn't have them happening in front of the guests. 'We have the photos to get through.'

'Forget the photos,' Ezekiel said. 'What do we need photos for?'

'The papers, apart from anything else,' Isabella

answered promptly. 'This is still the wedding of
the season, regardless of who actually got married.' Her voice dropped low for the last half of
the sentence and Helena winced.

Photos. Helena's smile slipped at the thought
until Isabella glared at her and she forced it back
into place. Where apparently it would stay for
the next hour or more, while the semi-famous
photographer Isabella had flown over from the
States took endless shots of her and Flynn looking happy and slightly shell-shocked.

Oh, well. Wasn't that how all brides and
grooms looked on their wedding day?

An hour of endless fake smiles later, Helena's
face ached. Still, photos over and done with, she
kissed the cheek of the next guest in the reception
line, wishing she'd made everyone wear name
tags for the occasion. She might know the guest
list backwards after helping to put it together, but
putting faces to those memorised names was another matter entirely.

Thea would have known them, though. Thea
would have wined and dined them as clients in
the past, would already have asked them questions about their kids or their pets. No wonder
they were all looking at Helena with such confusion and curiosity. She wasn't what they'd expected, or wanted.

She was kind of used to that.

Beside her, Flynn seemed totally at ease, chatting happily with every person who came past. He, at least, seemed pleased with how the day had turned out.

'Such a beautiful day,' a woman in a green hat said, fake smile making it clear that she might well be talking about the weather rather than the wedding.

'Wasn't it?' Isabella said, ignoring the false undertone. 'We're all just so delighted to be one happy family at last.'

'I'm sure,' Mrs Green Hat replied. 'Although you do seem to be missing a couple of members right now!'

Isabella's tinkling laugh gave away nothing. 'Oh, well, we have everyone who really matters right here, don't we?'

'I suppose so. Except you do seem to be missing a best man, at least.' Good grief, the woman was relentless! 'I heard Zeke was home for the wedding, and I was so looking forward to seeing him. Such a bright young man.'

Isabella's expression froze at that, her grin nudging towards a rictus. Leaning between them, Helena plastered on what she hoped was an apologetic smile. 'I'm so sorry to hurry you along, but I'm afraid the line is already out of the door and people are more than ready for the wedding breakfast, I'm sure. Perhaps you and Isabella can catch up a little later?'

Mrs Green Hat looked a little sour at the interruption, as if too much lemon had been squeezed in her gin and tonic, but she nodded politely anyway. No one argued with the bride on her wedding day, did they?

'Of course. Isabella, I look forward to talking with you and *both* your sons later.' She stalked off towards the dining room, not even bothering to acknowledge Thomas at the end of the line, which Helena thought was just plain *rude,* thank you very much. Although, quite honestly, Thomas probably deserved it today. But Mrs Green Hat didn't know that.

Now, if she'd avoided Ezekiel, who continued to glower at every single person he spoke to, she could understand it.

It took forever, but eventually the last of the guests paraded past them and into the dining room. Ezekiel immediately disappeared in the direction of his study without so much as a by-your-leave, but Helena wasn't complaining.

In fact, she let out a sigh of relief and slipped her feet out of her heels for a moment, letting the cool stone floor soothe her toes.

'I don't understand why Thea couldn't at least leave her shoes and veil if she had to run out on us at the last moment.' Isabella peered critically at the bright pink shoes lying on the floor. Thomas must have filled her in on the events of the day, Helena supposed. 'It would be common courtesy, really.'

Rather than not actually running out on her wedding in the first place, Helena supposed. Isabella always did obsess about the details. It wasn't the first time she'd missed the big picture because of it.

'I like the pink ones,' she said, partly just to annoy her new mother-in-law.

'So do I, actually,' Flynn said, standing beside her, and she flashed him a huge smile. Maybe this was why people got married—to have someone on their side when they had to deal with their parents. She'd heard of worse reasons.

Thomas, with a weary sigh, lowered himself into an armchair at the edge of the hallway. 'I suppose we should have known. It's not like she didn't have form. I wonder where they are now.' He stared out of the open front door as he spoke and Helena couldn't help but follow his gaze.

'Zeke and Thea?' Isabella asked. 'God only knows. Probably off somewhere trying to find new ways to destroy our family.'

'They were in love,' Helena said, without even realising she planned to say it. 'They wanted to be together. And we thought…well, we thought this was the best option. Flynn and I.' She reached for him blindly, relieved when Flynn grabbed her hand and held it tight.

'We did,' he agreed. 'Still do, actually.'

Isabella studied her so intently that Helena stared at her toes to avoid her gaze. Her pedicure was the exact same colour as her shoes, she realised with pleasure. She almost wanted to point it out to her mother-in-law, to prove that she was good at details, too.

'Maybe you were right,' Isabella said finally. 'It might all be for the best. At least you're less likely to make a dramatic scene than your sister. If it hadn't been for Thea's place in the company...well, I might have suggested to Ezekiel that he pick you for Flynn instead. I said as much to Thea, actually. So I suppose she knew she had a stand-in, if she needed it.'

'Mother,' Flynn said, the hint of warning in his voice enough to make Isabella stop talking.

But it couldn't stop the icy fingers that crept up the back of Helena's neck at her words. She tugged her hand free from Flynn's. It wasn't just Isabella making it perfectly clear that Helena was second choice, a last resort. She already knew that, thanks. But had Thea really known what would happen? Helena thought not. But it seemed, however cross Ezekiel might be, Isabella wasn't too disappointed with this turn of events. Why would she be? She got a docile, eager to please wife for her son. Flynn had probably been overjoyed when she'd suggested it.

Except, of course, he knew that it was potentially only temporary. Isabella didn't.

But it was only a matter of time before she found out.

Flynn's hand felt suddenly cold without Helena's in it. Curse his mother. Wasn't it enough that *he* had to know that he was an unfortunate backup plan without her driving it home that his new bride was in exactly the same position?

It was time to get the focus back where it belonged—on *their* marriage, rather than the one that hadn't happened.

'Is that all the guests in?' he asked.

'Finally, yes,' Helena said with a small hint of a smile, as if she knew what he was trying to do.

'God only knows how much wine they'll have got through already.' Isabella tucked her hand through Thomas's arm. 'We'll go in and take our seats, then the steward can come and announce you. Is your father coming back?' The last part was added almost as an afterthought, Flynn realised. While Ezekiel might believe this whole day was all about him and his company, as far as Isabella was concerned, this was a social occasion presided over by herself and Thomas. The man she'd never quite left her husband for, but who was more of a husband to her anyway.

Wow, his family was screwed up.

'I'm sure he'll come through eventually,' Flynn said, even though Ezekiel hadn't even mentioned he was leaving, let alone returning to the festivities. It would be just like his father to spite them all after having his plans meddled with. Flynn was pretty certain that, actually, Ezekiel would be perfectly content with Helena as a daughter-in-law. It was just the fact that he hadn't been consulted, or had the final say in the matter, that rankled the old man.

Thomas and Isabella made their way through to the dining room and, rather suddenly, Flynn was alone with his wife for the first time since they'd decided to go through with the marriage. No, not the marriage. That still hadn't been decided, and wouldn't be until they had a document rather more legally binding than a scrawled-on invitation with the wrong name on the front. The wedding, then. That much, at least, they had certainly gone through with.

That much had paperwork.

'I'm sorry about that,' he said apologetically. 'You know my mother.'

'Rather too well,' Helena agreed, and he couldn't help but smile.

'Yes, well. How did you cope with your first

official event as an Ashton—the receiving line, I mean? It seemed to go pretty smoothly to me.'

'Yeah, it was fine, mostly. There were a couple of extra-nosy people asking about Zeke—not Thea, of course, that would be too obvious. Your mother and I put them off, for now anyway.' She sighed. 'Although I dread to think what sort of questions they'll be ready to ask after a few too many glasses of champagne.'

She was right, Flynn realised. Sheer politeness might have stopped the bulk of the comments and observations in the church itself, but once the speeches were over all bets would be off.

Which meant the speeches would have to be something quite spectacular, to give them something else to talk about. Or something else to believe, about the way this day had gone.

'We have to change the story,' he said, and Helena's smile turned awkward.

'You got that from Thea,' she said when he raised an eyebrow. 'That's one of her big PR phrases.'

'Well, it applies today. We need to change people's perceptions of what happened here today.' And quickly, since he could already see the steward coming to fetch them.

'Like the fact you married the wrong woman?'

'Exactly that.'

The steward moved to open the door and Hel-

ena grabbed Flynn's arm as she slipped her slim
feet back into those bright pink shoes.

'Any idea how?' she murmured, as the dining room doors opened and the steward stepped
through.

'One or two,' Flynn muttered back.

'Like?'

But then the steward was announcing them as
Mr and Mrs Flynn Ashton, and the show was on
again. Helena would just have to wait and see.
Flynn smiled to himself. Fixing this could be his
wedding present to her.

CHAPTER THREE

IT WAS HARD not to be a little bitter. Helena had spent weeks choosing the perfect menu for this dinner, along with Isabella and the wedding planner and even Thea when she'd had time. They'd tasted and sampled all kinds of dishes, weighed up the pros and cons of a fish course against a sorbet between courses, and debated the merits of local versus imported cheeses for hours. And now, here she was, sitting right in the middle of the top table—and she'd barely tasted a mouthful of any of the plates put in front of her.

It wasn't that she didn't want to eat. She was starving, as it happened. But the very efficiently tied corset laces were starting to make breathing a bit more of an issue than she'd like, and she didn't want to strain them any more than she had to.

She stared longingly at the dessert in front of her and resigned herself to just a small taste. And to staying away from the champagne. Bubbles always went straight to her head, and on an empty stomach they'd be disastrous. Especially today. Today, she needed all of her faculties about her.

'Are you okay? You're looking kind of…pink,' Flynn asked, leaning in. Helena supposed to the crowds of guests it looked as if he was murmuring sweet nothings in his bride's ear. Not asking her why her complexion had coloured to match her shoes.

'It's the corset. It was okay standing up but now it's kind of…binding.' Which it was supposed to be, really. It was just that Helena was so very fond of oxygen. And dessert.

Flynn didn't answer immediately. Helena glanced up to see his cheeks approaching shoe colour, too. 'I'm sorry. Do you want me to…?' He trailed off, waving a hand behind her back.

Helena shook her head. 'Too late now. It'll be fine. I just need to make it through the speeches then I'll escape and find a maid or someone to adjust it.'

'Just don't let any of the guests see you.' Flynn flashed her a quick grin. 'You'll have the rumour mill announcing you're pregnant in no time.'

Pregnant. Of course. Because she was married now. And that was what married women did, wasn't it? Gave their husbands babies.

Isabella probably wouldn't even cry and send her away this time.

This time, it wouldn't be a scandal, a shameful thing. It would be wanted, loved. Kept.

And the fact it might break her heart again still wouldn't matter.

A waiter reached in to clear her barely touched plate and Helena murmured a thank you, more grateful for the interruption to her thoughts than the service.

'Time for the speeches next,' she said, visualising the timetable for the day as she'd seen it on the wedding planner's clipboard.

'And your dad's up first. At least he always makes a good speech.'

Helena stared at him in disbelief, but Flynn appeared utterly unaware of what he'd said. 'A good speech?'

'Well, yeah.' Flynn shrugged. 'Doesn't he? I mean, he does all those charity event speaker things, and he always talks well to the board. And I thought he did pretty well last night, at the rehearsal dinner.'

Helena shook her head. 'No wonder Thea slept with Zeke,' she muttered. After listening to their father's speech about her the night before—including, amongst other things, a line about how glad he was that, by agreeing to marry Flynn, Thea had finally made a decision in her personal life as good as the ones she made in business—even Helena had been ready to flee the room.

And Flynn hadn't even noticed that his fiancée might have been a bit upset.

She wondered what little gems Dad would have in store for her. Assuming that he'd taken the time to rewrite it from his original speech, as planned for Thea. He might not. They seemed fairly interchangeable to him today—neither one of his daughters living up to what he wanted or expected from them.

She didn't have to wait long to find out. The moment the last of the plates were cleared, Thomas Morrison was on his feet, carefully clinking the silverware against a champagne flute.

'Ladies and gentlemen, friends and family, welcome—welcome to you all!' Thomas smiled broadly around at the assembled company, and Helena wondered exactly how much of the champagne he'd had that afternoon.

'On this very special day, I'd like to thank you all for travelling to be with us, not just on my own behalf, but on behalf of my dear old friends, Ezekiel and Isabella, too. I know that they feel, as I do, that this day would not have been so magical without all of you here to share it.'

Pause for applause. Flynn did have a point, although she'd never admit as much. Her father knew how to play a crowd.

It was just a shame he didn't know how to make his own daughters feel as special.

'This day, this joining of our two families, has been long coming, and long desired. Not just for the obvious reasons of business—although I know several of you very pleased to see your stocks and shares safe for another generation!' Laughter, mostly from a table of middle-aged men in pinstriped suits with much younger wives towards the back of the room. 'No, I have far greater reasons for wanting to see our families irrevocably linked.'

Helena swallowed at the word *irrevocably*, and felt Flynn flinch beside her. Was he thinking about how to get out of this marriage, like she was? Or was he plotting how to keep her in it?

'Helena, my Helena, has always been my golden child. My baby girl. And to see her safe and secure with a man such as Flynn, a man I already trusted with my company, is quite frankly a joy!'

If her cheeks had been pink from oxygen deprivation before, then they had to be bright red and clashing with her shoes by now. As she stared at her full champagne glass, watching the bubbles rise and pop, Flynn sneaked his hand into hers and she squeezed gratefully.

'Flynn—' Thomas turned to address his new son-in-law directly '—you have been given a precious gift today. I expect you to take very good care of it.'

'I will, sir.' Flynn's voice was sure and certain, and the whole room burst into applause again at the sound of it.

'Okay, maybe he's not dreadful at speeches,' Helena murmured to Flynn but, even as she said it, Thomas launched into a long, overdone thank you speech to Isabella for all she'd done in helping to raise her and organise the day. 'Sometimes.'

'Wait until you hear mine,' Flynn teased. But Helena tensed at the very idea. What on earth was he going to say? *Hi, guys, I know you came to see me marry that other girl but, hey, change of plan and, under the circumstances, this was the best I could do. More champagne, anyone?*

'*This* you're worried about?' Flynn asked, his voice low but amazed. 'Marrying a guy you never even considered as a possible date on no notice in someone else's wedding dress, fine. But the thought of me making a speech makes you tense up? You don't need the corset, your shoulders are so rigid.'

'Not the thought of you making a speech. The thought of you adapting a speech about Thea to suit me on the spot. The fact that everyone here will know you're actually talking about another woman.'

Flynn didn't reply immediately, and when Helena looked up his expression was thoughtful. 'Just wait and listen,' he said finally, just as Thomas asked the room to be upstanding for the bride and groom.

'To Flynn and Helena!' She supposed she should just be glad that most people managed to get her name right.

Flynn got to his feet as everyone else sat down, and Helena gave up worrying about the tightness of her corset laces. It wasn't as if she could breathe while this was going on anyway.

'It's traditional, I know, for the groom to toast the bridesmaids,' he started.

Helena winced instinctively. *That's right— draw attention to exactly what's untraditional about this wedding.*

'But, as you might have noticed, my wife and I don't actually have any today.'

A nervous laugh, and not even the usual cheer at the use of 'my wife and I'. Yeah, this was going to go *brilliantly.*

'A lot of things about today's wedding might not have been exactly as people were expecting. But, in fact, everything is just as it should be.'

He smiled down at her and something in Helena's chest loosened, for the first time that day.

'All along, we knew we wanted to join our families together, to go into the future as a pair, a team. We wanted to secure our future, and our future happiness. But you can't make a plan for love; you can't schedule romance and desire. You can't outsmart Cupid, as Helena and I learned.'

It was all true, Helena realised. Everything he was saying accurately described Thea and Zeke's discoveries and disappointments of the last couple of days. But the way he said it, the way he smiled lovingly at her as he spoke…it was as if he were telling a different story altogether.

Their story.

'Duty is one thing; family duty something altogether heavier. But true love…well, true love trumps them all.' Women were 'aahing' around the tables, and Helena thought she might even have seen one of the middle-aged men in the pinstriped suits wipe at his eyes. How was Flynn doing this?

'I truly believe that our wedding today is just the first stop on a journey of a lifetime. With Helena, I feel like I have come home at last. Together we, and our families, have a wonderful future ahead of us. And I couldn't be prouder to have my wife by my side as we venture into it.'

Flynn tugged her up to stand beside him, one arm wrapped around her waist, and raised his glass. 'To Helena,' he said, and the room echoed with the repeats.

And just for a moment, standing there in her

sister's too tight wedding dress with the wrong shoes pinching her feet, Helena could see the future Thea had planned for herself. A future of acceptance and appreciation, having a man beside her who always managed to say the right thing at the right time.

It almost seemed like the fairy tale it was supposed to be. For a moment, anyway. Until her guests started calling for something more.

'Kiss her!' Mr Teary-Pinstripes called. 'Kiss, kiss, kiss, kiss!' The rest of his table picked up the chant. Then the rest of the room.

Suddenly, Helena almost wished the corset *was* tight enough to make her faint.

Imagining a fairy tale future wasn't the same as kissing the prince. This wasn't how it was supposed to go. They'd managed to avoid it in the church, where at least it would have been expected to be a chaste and swift kiss. Here, now, after all the wine and the toasts…these people wanted the real thing, and anything less was only going to start up rumours again.

She couldn't let that happen. Not after Flynn's speech had tidied away all the talk so neatly.

If they wanted a kiss, she was going to have to give it to them.

She turned to Flynn, eyebrows raised, and he echoed the gesture. 'I never thought my first kiss with my husband would be quite so public,' she murmured, quiet enough that she knew it wouldn't be heard over the chanting.

'It's just for show.' He flashed her a quick smile.

Just a show. Of course. They weren't really in love, whatever Flynn had suggested in his speech. This marriage was only temporary, just until they could sort everything out. It wouldn't—couldn't—last. Not when she couldn't give Flynn what he wanted most.

None of which explained why there seemed to be too much blood in her veins, or why she couldn't look away from Flynn's caramel-brown eyes as he smiled down at her.

Helena's heart raced as he wrapped an arm around her waist and pulled her close, the chanting turning to cheering around them.

It's just for show. The words spun in her head, but all Helena could think as Flynn bent in to kiss her was: *If this is just a show, how am I going to survive the real thing?*

Just a show. That was the key.

Except it wasn't.

Yes, the only reason his first kiss with his wife was taking place in front of a captive audience was to prove a point—to show them that Helena wasn't some sort of poor consolation prize.

But that wasn't enough. He had to show *Helena* that too.

And Helena knew the truth.

If he wanted her to stick with this—to believe they had a real future together—well, that future had to start right now. With their first kiss.

'Kiss, kiss, kiss, kiss!' The chanting around them faded into nothing as he leant in closer, his eyes closing as his lips brushed against hers, softly at first, not wanting to spook her. But then, oh, then… Flynn's fingers clutched at her hip, the silk of her dress slipping against his skin as he deepened the kiss.

She tasted like champagne and gold, expensive and sparkling, her mouth warm and willing under his. He'd wanted to prove a point with this kiss but, for the life of him, he couldn't remember what it was. All he could think about was how soft her body was against his, how perfectly it fitted to him.

He opened his eyes, wanting to drink in the sight of her too, wanting to see her reaction, to know if she was as affected as him. But Helena's eyes were closed and, along with his vision, his hearing seemed to return too—or at least his awareness of it.

The chanting had turned to cheering—when, Flynn didn't know. But he was suddenly aware that he was making a spectacle of himself—and

Helena—by falling so completely into what was supposed to be a simple kiss. Just a moment to appease the crowd, and a promise of what could follow later.

If their first kiss had knocked him senseless, what would their second do to him? Never mind their third and fourth...

Reluctantly, Flynn loosened his hold on his wife and pulled back, just enough to signal to Helena that the kiss was over. Her eyelids fluttered open and Flynn was gratified to see misty confusion in her bluebell bright eyes, too. At least he wasn't the only one losing his mind over a kiss.

'Well,' Isabella said in a low voice as they pulled apart, 'at least no one here is left in any doubt that you both got what you wanted out of this arrangement.' Flynn couldn't tell if his mother disapproved of that or not. It was often hard to tell with Isabella. He found it easiest to assume that she did disapprove, most of the time.

Not that it made any difference now. He was married to Helena and there was nothing anyone could do about that.

The cheering had turned to chatter and laughter now, after a smattering of applause. Helena's cheeks were pink as she sat down, and Flynn flattered himself that the blush had less to do with her corset than it had.

'Nearly there now,' he murmured to her, reaching to take her hand. She let him hold it long enough for a reassuring squeeze then tugged it away again, giving him a polite, but non-committal, smile.

Flynn frowned. What had changed? She'd been right there with him in that kiss, he could tell. So why the cool distance now?

As the guests finished their coffees and headed through to the adjoining room, where a bar had been set up for them while the band set up on the terrace, Flynn studied his bride as she sipped tea, and considered.

Helena had been instrumental in the wedding planning, but she hadn't been part of the prenuptial contract discussions. But she *was* Thea's sister. They'd have talked about the terms of the agreement, surely? Which meant that Helena probably knew that marital relations hadn't been contractually required for the first couple of years. Thea had wanted time to settle into married life, and to continue to build up her career, before they started a family. And, since they weren't in love, or even in lust, sex wasn't really necessary until then. At least, on paper.

There was a firm fidelity clause, though. And Thea had changed her mind, just two nights ago, about what she wanted from the marriage in physical terms. She'd wanted them to get to know each other as man and wife, and have that time together first before kids.

Although how much that decision had to do with her trying to hide her feelings for his brother, Flynn suspected he was better off not knowing.

Still, maybe she hadn't discussed that change of plans with Helena. And, even if she had, there was no contract between Helena and him. No carefully debated and worded agreement, no consensus of opinion. Just confusion, lack of clarity and the potential for miscommunication.

This was why the world needed paperwork.

He'd have to talk to her, discuss the situation and what they wanted to happen next. It was useful to have a good idea of their individual needs before they got the solicitors involved, or at least that was what he'd found with her sister.

But that would have to wait until he got her alone. And with two hundred wedding guests still watching them closely—either waiting for another kiss or some sign of what really went down that morning—Flynn didn't see that happening very soon.

A smile crept on to his face as a thought occurred to him. There was one chance for them to be almost alone, if still observed, very soon indeed.

'What are you smiling at?' Helena asked from beside him.

'I'm just looking forward to our first dance,' he answered honestly.

'Well, it can't be any more of a spectacle than our first kiss.' Helena covered her eyes for a moment, obviously embarrassed.

'Don't knock the kiss,' Flynn said, leaning back in his chair. 'I think that kiss might set the tone for our whole marriage.'

Helena's gaze flashed up to his face, uncertainty in her eyes. Flynn tried to give her a reassuring look. She'd feel better once they'd agreed terms. And he'd feel better once he knew she was in this for the long haul. He could persuade her that sticking with the marriage was better for everybody, he was sure.

Even if he had to kiss her a hundred more times to convince her.

'And now, please welcome Mr and Mrs Flynn Ashton on to the floor for their first dance!'

Helena thought her face might crack from all the smiling. Still, she tried to keep up the ecstatically happy bride act as she took Flynn's hand and stepped out into the middle of the ballroom. How had Isabella even managed to *find* a villa with a ballroom? The woman had to have ridiculous magical abilities or something.

Helena just hoped she'd use her powers for good.

'You okay?' Flynn asked as the band struck up the first notes of the first dance. *It Had to Be You*. Thea had picked it after glancing over the band's set list, and Helena still wasn't sure if she'd meant it as a joke. Except Thea wasn't stuck dancing to it for the next three and a half minutes or whatever. Helena was.

'I'm fine.' She smiled up at her husband and hoped he wouldn't notice she was lying. She was a long way from fine.

It was the kiss that had started it. The kiss that had left her knees weak and her brain foggy. Followed by all the sincere congratulations that no one had offered *before* Flynn's speech and a roomful of strangers telling her how this must be the happiest day of her life.

Helena was pretty sure it would go down forever as the most bizarre and confusing. But *happiest*? That really wasn't the right word for it.

Flynn led her around the dance floor without her even having to think about where her feet went next, as if he had a diagram in his head that he just had to follow and everything would be graceful and perfect. Which, actually, knowing Flynn, he probably did.

'So,' he said as the singer launched into the second verse, 'I think we made it through the day without disaster.'

'I guess we did.' After the dancing, all that was

left was the sending off. Except she and Flynn weren't going anywhere except upstairs to bed.

Bed.

Oh.

Where were they going to sleep? The bridal suite Thea had been using, which would have been set up for a romantic wedding night while they were all down at the chapel? Or the smaller room Helena had taken as her own? Or even Flynn's room at the far end of the villa?

And, more importantly, was Flynn expecting that they'd be going to bed *together*?

'About that,' she said, stumbling a little as her shoe got stuck in the too-long hem of her dress. Flynn caught her, strong hands keeping her upright and even still dancing as she found her balance. 'I mean, about making it through the day. And to the night. Um...'

Flynn gave a low chuckle that somehow sounded dirtier than she'd ever imagined he was capable of. 'Don't worry. I don't think anyone is going to be sober enough to notice where either of us sleep tonight. Why don't you take the bridal suite, just in case anyone checks, and I'll stick with my room? I'll have work to do in the morning anyway, and my laptop and files are all set up in there.'

Of course. Work.

Just when she was starting to think that Flynn

was a little more enthusiastic about this wedding than she'd expected. But no, it was all just the show, the spectacle, still.

Except that kiss hadn't felt like a show. It had definitely been a spectacle, but it had felt…real. Tingly.

But she wasn't supposed to be getting tingly feelings about this man. Her husband. Stupid as it seemed. She needed to keep this business-like and official until they could sit down and agree a way to get out of it. As she'd told him that morning, this didn't have to be forever.

Couldn't be forever.

If she didn't end this early enough, she'd have to tell him everything, sooner or later. Explain why she couldn't give him all the things he wanted. Had Isabella already realised? Was that why she'd looked so frustrated all day, whenever no one important had been looking?

The band launched into a repeat of the last verse, and Flynn spun her round with a little more enthusiasm. Not enough to be called abandon, of course. And probably planned ahead of time. But the crowd cheered anyway, and Helena tried to improve her mood with the knowledge that this was nearly all over. Another hour or so and they'd serve the cake and light supper buffet, even though no one could possibly be hungry again after the dinner they'd just eaten—except her. And she still couldn't eat because of the ridiculous corset.

Maybe she could smuggle a doggy bag upstairs under her skirts...

The band came to a triumphant finish and Flynn dipped her low over his arm. Helena's heel slid against the wooden floor for a second, then held. Heart racing, she looked up into her husband's eyes and realised her heart wasn't going to slow down any time soon.

Polite applause echoed in her ears as Flynn's smile—a slow private one she wasn't used to—spread across his face and she realised that she was still half upside down with her hair threatening to break free from its pins.

Deliberately, he raised her up to standing again, but his arm tight around her waist kept her upright. Her mind spun—from the dance, from the dip, but mostly from the realisation that she'd thought Flynn was about to kiss her again. Had expected it, almost as her due.

Had wanted it.

And that was dangerous.

With a tight smile, she shuffled back out of his arms. Flynn let her go easily and she tried to stamp down the small swell of disappointment she felt at that.

'I think my father has the next dance,' she said as the band struck up the next tune.

'Of course,' Flynn replied, still smiling. 'And who are we to mess with tradition?'

'Who, indeed?' Helena twirled away, hitching her dress up a little to avoid tripping, and went to find her father. He might not always be her favourite person but he was a great deal safer to be around than her husband right now.

Several hours and considerably more dances later, the evening finally approached its end. Helena had thought about staging a grand departure earlier, but realised that would leave her alone in the bridal suite with her husband and two hundred people downstairs listening for signs of the marriage being consummated.

So not happening.

But at midnight the coaches and cars arrived like carriages on the driveway and the staff efficiently and discreetly persuaded everyone out of the door. Most were staying at hotels down in the town where there would be bars they could abuse all they wanted. But not here.

A few close family and friends of Isabella's *were* staying at the villa, but Helena was optimistic they could avoid them tonight. The bridal suite was at one far end of a wing, with her own bedroom, her father's and Isabella and Ezekiel's suite between it and the rest of the villa. Zeke and Flynn had been roomed at the other end of the building but maybe she could persuade Flynn to take her old room. She could get someone to move his work stuff over now, while no one was looking. It would be much easier to keep up the illusion that they were actually sharing the bridal suite that way.

Helena smiled a gracious goodbye at a passing flurry of guests, then moved away to explain her plan to Flynn—only to see him exiting the room behind her father and his. Where were they all going?

Frowning, she made to follow and find out, but stopped when a hand slipped through the crook of her arm. To the departing guests, it probably looked like a motherly gesture from her new mother-in-law, but Helena knew differently. Isabella had a grip of steel and if she didn't want Helena going after Flynn she didn't stand a chance of making it.

'Where are the menfolk off to?' Helena asked in what she hoped was an unconcerned tone.

'I believe that Ezekiel and Thomas had some details to hammer out with Flynn, after today's… occurrences.' Helena had never heard a wedding sound so inconvenient.

'Details? What sort of details?'

Isabella waved the hand that wasn't gripping Helena's arm as if to say it was nothing for Helena to worry her pretty little head about. Except

Helena did worry. Would worry. Was currently worrying. Pretty much in every tense—especially since she knew beyond any doubt that the three men would be talking about her.

No, not just talking about her. Planning her life. Without any input from her.

'Just little things, I'm sure,' Isabella said lightly. 'Probably what adjustments need to be made to the original marriage contract, for one.'

Yeah, because that wasn't a big thing at all.

'Don't you think I should be in there for that?' Helena asked.

Isabella gave her a disparaging look. 'I can't imagine it would make much of a difference.' Which was, depressingly, very true. But it didn't mean she wouldn't like the opportunity to say her part.

The door had closed behind the men and Helena knew any chance she had of gate-crashing their summit meeting had passed. All she could do now was wait to see what they decided about her future.

And then choose whether or not she was willing to go along with it.

She allowed herself a small secret smile. They could plan all they wanted, but they weren't in charge of her life. Flynn might be her husband, but he didn't own her. And she hadn't signed any paperwork promising him anything.

Her future was her own and she wouldn't let the men in her life tell her what to do with it.

'I'm going to go up to the bridal suite,' she told Isabella in a sweet, not-causing-any-trouble-here tone. 'It *is* my wedding night, after all.'

'Of course.' Isabella loosened her hold on Helena's arm, studying her face. Helena kept her expression bland. 'I'm sure Flynn won't keep you waiting too long.'

Only until tomorrow morning, given the conversation they'd had while they danced. But her mother-in-law didn't need to know that. 'Well, I'd better go and get ready for him, then.' With a smile, she turned to leave the room, planning to snag a maid to move Flynn's things on her way.

'Helena.' She turned back at Isabella's call. Flynn's mother had a small crease between her eyebrows, as if she were still trying to make sense of everything that had happened that day. Maybe she was. God knew it didn't make any sense to Helena yet, and most of it had been her idea. 'I just wanted to say…maybe things have worked out for the best, after all. Maybe this can be a fresh start for you and Flynn. For you, especially.'

Helena's polite smile tightened until her cheeks ached. 'I hope so,' she said, not even sure if she was lying or not. 'It's about time I was given a second chance around here.'

And, with that, she turned and swept out of the ballroom, leaving her wedding day behind her.

It was time for the wedding night.

CHAPTER FOUR

'WELL. THAT WAS a day.' Thomas Morrison collapsed into one of the wing chairs by the fire of Ezekiel's study. 'Tell me you keep the good brandy in here, old friend?'

'Of course I do,' Ezekiel answered, his tone irritable. 'Flynn?'

As his father settled himself into the other wing chair, Flynn moved to the hidden drinks cabinet Ezekiel had found within the first thirty minutes of occupying the office and pulled out three of the good glasses. He deserved a drink, after today. More than just a sip of champagne or half a glass of wine with dinner. He'd held it together all day long, turned a potential disaster into a victory, and now he was about to be cross-examined on his actions by his father and father-in-law.

He was *owed* this brandy.

'So.' Ezekiel studied him as Flynn handed out the brandies, placing his own on the low table between them as he dragged another chair over. 'You're a married man now.'

'My son-in-law,' Thomas added, as if either of these facts might have eluded Flynn so far that day.

'This is true.' Sitting, Flynn stretched his long legs out in front of him, feeling the aches from standing too long in thin-soled shoes. Brandy would help with those too, he decided.

'So perhaps you would care to explain *exactly* what you were thinking?' Ezekiel's icy tone would have made a weaker man shiver, but Flynn was used to it. Obviously the old man had been working up to this all day. Better to let him get it out.

'I was thinking about the best course of action in an unfortunate situation.' Flynn kept his gaze steadily on his father's face as he spoke.

'We had a plan! We had a contract, signed and agreed, ready to come into force the moment the girl said "I do"! Now what do we have? A dumb blonde who knows nothing about the company, who can't provide the PR boost we needed, and who you married without a pre-nup so will probably run off with some footballer or something before you even reach your first anniversary!' Ezekiel turned briefly towards Thomas. 'No offence.'

Helena's father merely shrugged. 'None taken. Helena has never been the most reliable of my daughters. But, you have to admit, she did step up today.'

'Yes, she did. And we'd be in a far worse position if she hadn't.' Flynn rubbed a hand across his forehead, suddenly tired. 'Look. Helena has agreed to negotiate a new marriage contract the moment the guests are gone and the buzz dies down. Beyond that…perhaps she doesn't have Thea's business skills, but she has other talents.'

'I bet she does,' Ezekiel muttered darkly. Flynn ignored the implication.

'She's a great hostess, very personable and appealing. And, most importantly, she has the best interests of our families, and the company, at heart. It was her idea to stand in for Thea this morning. She wanted to protect her sister's reputation and preserve this whole wedding of the year spectacle.' Of course, she'd also wanted to avoid having to tell their parents what had happened to Thea and Zeke. Something Flynn had great sympathy with.

'Ah, yes, her sister.' Ezekiel sat back in his chair, fingers steepled in front of him. 'At some point we need to discuss what happened to the unreliable Thea. But what's done is done. What matters now is what we do next. Thomas? What do you think?'

Thomas sighed as he contemplated his daughter. Flynn's jaw clenched at the sound of it.

'Helena's a good girl, mostly. Had her moments, of course, but I hope that we're past those now. Isabella thinks that maybe that's why she took Thea's place. To prove she was ready to put the past behind her.'

'Does she?' Ezekiel nodded. 'Good insight, that woman. One of the reasons I married her.'

And still he didn't find it strange that his wife discussed this with his business partner, not himself, Flynn thought. The relationships between his and Helena's parents still baffled him.

He frowned as Thomas's words sank in. 'What past? What happened?' What was he missing here? His memories of Helena were of the sweet golden child Thomas had talked about in his speech. Maybe she seemed a little more prickly these days, underneath that smooth and charming surface, but Flynn had never really been close enough to investigate further.

He would have to investigate now, though. And he needed all the intelligence he could get going into that.

But apparently he wasn't going to get it tonight.

'Nothing that needs to worry you now, son.' Thomas gave him a kind smile and Flynn tried not to flinch at his use of the word 'son' as an endearment. Ezekiel had never managed that. Not once in thirty years. But then, Thomas had always wanted a son and never got one. Ezekiel had longed for one then got two by accident.

How could he have ever hoped to compete with biology?

'An heir and a spare; that's what a man needs.' The words echoed in Flynn's head from nearly twenty years ago. His father, in another study, with a different glass in his hand, still handing down pronouncements and never, ever listening. *'But you don't ever want to have to use the spare, if you can avoid it. And in this case...well, blood is blood. And yours isn't mine.'*

He remembered the moment so clearly. He'd always known he was adopted; no one had even tried to hide it. But standing there in front of his father as he'd explained exactly why Flynn would never matter, would never be good enough, would never truly count...he could still feel the stabbing pains in his heart now, so many years later.

Flynn rubbed absently at his chest as his father set down his brandy glass on the table and prepared to pass judgement.

'She'll do as she's told,' Ezekiel pronounced. 'And if she doesn't...well, you can always get her pregnant. That tends to calm a woman down. Just make sure she signs the papers before the child is born!' His father's wheezy laugh rattled through him like a curse, and Thomas joined in after only a moment.

I can't sleep with her, Flynn thought, trying to keep his horrified disgust to himself, even as the bile rose up in his throat. It might be the obvious way to keep Helena at his side—crushing any chance of an annulment, for a start, and bringing them together, showing her that there could be something good between them. Something that could maybe even grow into love.

But it wouldn't be fair. He wasn't his father, or even hers. He wouldn't trap her that way until they had some ground rules down. And as much as he wanted a child, an heir of his own, he needed the plan in place before that happened. No child of his would be used as a tool or a weapon.

Not like Ezekiel had used him and Zeke.

'I think I know how to handle my own wife.' Flynn tried to sound amused, confident and true, even though it was a complete lie. Thea, he'd have known how to handle. He'd done the background research, spent time with her, made sure to discuss everything they needed to know about each other.

Except, apparently, the fact that she was in love with his brother.

Still, that aside, he knew Thea. Helena he hadn't got a clue about.

But he was willing to learn. Had to learn, before he could let himself get close. Had to know if she'd stick with him, stand beside him hereafter, before he let himself believe in this marriage. Which meant keeping his hands off her—even after that kiss.

Ezekiel laughed again, sounding even creakier and wheezier than before. 'If you believe that, you're a bigger fool than I took you for. No man ever knows how to truly handle a woman. They thrive on being unpredictable. But you give it a go, if you like. You've got two weeks here on honeymoon together. Get her to sign something binding—the same general terms as we agreed for her sister—and I'll leave you alone to "handle" her. But if you haven't got the paperwork sorted by the time you come back to London, Thomas and I will take it over.'

Flynn's fist clenched against the arm of his chair and the other squeezed his glass so hard that a less expensive vessel would have cracked and smashed. This wasn't just the business they wanted to control. It was him and his future— and Helena's. He'd thought that Zeke forcing their father to name Flynn as CEO within the year would have meant he could finally take on the power and the role he was meant to have. Instead, he didn't even seem to have power over his own marriage.

But what else could he do? If he didn't manage to resolve things with Helena in two weeks he'd look weak anyway. And Flynn knew his father well enough to know he'd use that to his advantage somehow.

'I will do this,' he said, his voice firm and dark. 'Helena is my wife, this is my marriage, and my company before long. I don't need the two of you interfering like a couple of old women.'

The brandy had mellowed them, Flynn realised when they both laughed. Time was he'd have been punished for speaking in such a way. But the balance of power had changed now, whether they liked it or not. They couldn't keep him out, or under their control any longer.

'Then we'll leave you to get on with that,' Ezekiel said, getting to his feet. He placed his empty glass on the table, and Thomas followed suit. 'We're flying out in the morning, but I'm sure your mother will make sure we see you before we go.'

Flynn nodded. Morning wasn't far away now. Not long until it was just him, Helena and the elephant of a post-nup in the middle of the villa. He'd fix this. He had to.

Thomas raised a hand in parting and headed out, but Ezekiel paused in the doorway. 'Two weeks, Flynn. I expect those papers on my desk within twenty-four hours of your return to London, or I'll take steps.'

He closed the door behind him before Flynn could respond. Flynn stared around his father's study, at the inner sanctum that was almost, almost his, and thought about going to talk to his wife.

Then he got up and poured himself another brandy instead. One thing at a time, he decided. And tomorrow, once everyone else had gone, was plenty soon enough.

Especially as he had a sneaking suspicion that Helena wasn't going to like being handled one little bit.

The bridal suite was bigger than she remembered. Or maybe it just seemed smaller when Thea was in there with her. It hadn't even been so bad when the maid was there, loosening the laces of her corset and helping her to step out of the heavy wedding dress.

But now it was just her, alone with the dress hanging from the wardrobe door, and Helena didn't quite know what to do with herself.

A maid had moved her belongings in, presumably during the reception. Helena wondered whether the wedding planner had asked her to do that, or if it had been Isabella. She wondered where Thea's things had gone.

She wondered where Thea and Zeke were right now.

Shaking her head, Helena moved over to the chest of drawers under the window, looking for her nightwear. The third drawer she opened yielded results, and she pulled out the slippery satin negligee she'd packed in a ridiculous fit of optimism.

'Just in case,' Thea had said when they were packing together, back in London. *'You know, a high percentage of engaged people in a recent study said that they met their partners at a mutual friend's wedding. You never know who you might meet!'*

She'd known what Thea meant, though, by the suggestion. That it was time for Helena to move on. To start living that part of her life again. She'd never talked with her sister about the hours spent with the counsellor, talking through the memories, nodding meaninglessly as she was told she couldn't blame herself, that what had happened to her didn't have to define her life. But probably, in Thea's mind, it had been eight years and that was long enough to dwell.

How could she explain that knowing those things was one thing, and acting on them another entirely?

So instead she'd pointed out that the only people she was likely to meet at a Morrison-Ashton wedding were clients, most of whom were either already married or too married to their jobs for Helena to be interested in them.

And now look at her. Married to the almost

CEO of the family business, the man who put the 'work' in 'workaholic'. Perfect.

She shoved the fancy nightie back in the drawer and slammed it shut. Returning to drawer number two, she yanked out a pair of workout shorts and a T-shirt instead. It wasn't as if Flynn was going to get the chance to appreciate—or even see—whatever she wore to bed tonight anyway.

Flopping back on to her bed, Helena grabbed her phone from where the maid had helpfully plugged it in to charge and set it on the bedside table. As she stared at the dark screen, a wave of homesick longing flooded through her.

She wanted her sister.

She needed Thea there, to talk through all the craziness. She was the only person in the world who could possibly understand and maybe make sense of all the thoughts and feelings and fears whirling around in Helena's brain right now. Thea would yell, she was pretty sure, and tell her she was an idiot and she didn't have to do this. She'd probably cry and feel guilty, too.

But she'd help her fix it, one way or another.

With a sigh, Helena dropped the phone on the bed cover beside her. That, of course, was exactly why she couldn't phone Thea. For the first time in her life, Thea had chosen to go after what she wanted, what would make her happy, rather than staying behind and helping Helena, or the family, or the business. Helena couldn't jeopardise that by calling her now, throwing her back into the family lunacy. Thea was out and she was happy. And Helena was going to keep it that way.

Which meant she had to fix this herself.

Wrapping her arms around her middle, Helena pulled her knees up and turned on her side, small and insignificant in the oversized room. There was another reason not to tell Thea, of course. A horrible, sneaky, underhand reason. One Helena really hoped wasn't true, but she couldn't promise that, even to herself.

Did I plan for this to happen?

Thea would ask. Maybe not immediately, but eventually it would come up. Thea had to have known about the crippling crush Helena had nurtured for Flynn when they were teens. At fourteen or fifteen, he'd been all she could think about. He was kind, serious, and his eyes had mesmerised her. Not boring blue like hers, but pools of molten caramel. Helena had written embarrassingly awful poetry about his eyes. But, more than anything, he hadn't treated her like 'little Helena' the way everyone else did. He'd seen her as a real person, not just a silly child. A woman, even, with her own dreams and ideas. And he'd encouraged her to go after them.

Of course, he'd been six years older and already away at university then, home only for holidays and birthdays. Maybe that was part of it—he wasn't around her enough to be irritated by the little hanger-on, the way Thea and Zeke had been. It had also ensured that Flynn had remained completely oblivious to her affections. And Helena wasn't about to let him find out now.

But Thea must have realised. Isabella certainly had. And since that was still…before, she'd been sympathetic, even caring and protective of Helena's feelings.

That crush was a decade old, of course, but the thought still lingered. Had she manipulated things so that she was the one who ended up in the wedding dress? She didn't think so—and, even if she had, she didn't think Thea and Zeke would be complaining. But she'd certainly jumped into that dress quickly enough.

She'd told Flynn, and herself, that it was all to save face, to protect the family—even to protect Flynn from any embarrassment. But, at the heart of it, had she married him because a part of her had never truly moved on from that crippling teenage crush?

Helena wasn't sure.

But she knew a crush wasn't enough of a reason to stay married, and neither was family loyalty. Just as she'd told Thea. And she already knew she wouldn't be able to give Flynn the future he wanted.

Still…

Maybe it was the champagne talking or the lack of food, but Helena couldn't shake one lingering thought. Even if it wasn't forever…could she really pass up the opportunity to live out the wedding night her fourteen-year-old self had dreamed of so often?

Her stomach clenched at just the idea of it. Could she even try? Thea, the counsellor—everyone had told her she had to move on with her life. Had to open up to intimacy again. And she'd tried, of course she had, but it had never felt quite…safe.

Flynn was safe. A laugh bubbled up as she remembered her father calling him 'a safe pair of hands'. But he was right. Flynn would never hurt her, or make her do anything she didn't want. And he was enough of a gentleman that if she changed her mind she was pretty sure he'd not just let her go but never even mention it again.

And he was her husband. Even if she wouldn't—couldn't—give him children, she could give him this. Give them this. And didn't they deserve something good at the end of this horrendous day?

It would be good, she knew. Better than good. She might not have a lot to compare it to, but that kiss…she'd almost melted at his feet right then. How could anything that led on from that kiss be less than spectacular?

Helena swallowed, made herself sit up. This was the rest of her life, starting today. She'd done her part and now they were all even. She wasn't going to waste any more time trying to make up for things—she'd done everything that she could. And maybe she and Flynn wouldn't make this marriage last longer than it took the ink to dry on the divorce papers, but didn't that mean there was all the more reason to mark the occasion?

She was moving on from everything that had led them to this day. And sleeping with her husband would prove that.

Pushing herself up off the bed, Helena padded across to the chest of drawers and opened the third drawer again, holding the negligee up against her body for a moment as she summoned up every bit of courage she possessed.

Time for a fresh start.

Flynn was halfway through the second brandy when the knock came. He blinked, confused, for a moment. This was his father's study. Who would come looking for him here at long past midnight? And it felt so weird to be the one about to call for whomever it was to come in. As if he should be sitting on the other side of the big old desk, staring censoriously at someone.

A second knock. Flynn shook his head, blamed the brandy for his thoughts and said, 'Come in.'

The door creaked open, slow and loud, and Flynn put down his glass and sat up straight as Helena's blonde waves appeared around the edge of it.

'Oh, good,' she said with an unfamiliar smile. 'You're alone. This could have been embarrassing otherwise.'

'Embarrassing?' Flynn asked, confused. But then Helena stepped into the room and he understood all too well. 'Oh.'

The pale satin of her negligee clung to curves he'd barely realised she had until he'd glimpsed her in her underwear that morning. Somehow, even if this ensemble covered more, it seemed worse. He could almost make out the dark tips of her nipples through the thin fabric, and his whole body was suddenly heavy with desire.

Helena bit her lip and Flynn knew he should set her at her ease, reassure her about…something. But he couldn't find the words. Any words. Could barely remember the English language, in fact.

'So, I was sitting up in the bridal suite and I got to thinking.' Turning, she closed the door behind her and Flynn's eyes focused automatically on her bottom, lush and curved and perfectly highlighted by the satin. Oh, he was doomed.

'Thinking,' he repeated dumbly, very aware that he had absolutely no idea what was happening here and, given the circumstances, probably little chance of figuring it out even if she explained it in words of no greater than two syllables. 'Uh…what about?'

'Us, mostly.' Facing him again, she flashed him a smile—a bright and happy smile like he remembered from Helena of old. Helena at fourteen, following him around the house all Christmas Day, her new camera in hand. Except Helena at fourteen had worn taffeta dresses his mother picked out and had never, ever rendered him speechless like this.

'You mean the wedding?' Flynn asked, feeling proud of himself for managing that much in the face of satin nightwear.

'More…the marriage.' Moving over to the drinks cabinet he'd left open, Helena poured herself a brandy, then brought the bottle over to top up his glass. Because obviously what he needed at this point was *more* alcohol. The two brandies he'd already had appeared to have addled his mind completely.

Or maybe that was just her.

She sat down in his father's abandoned chair and crossed her legs, slim ankles showing under the hem of her negligee. Flynn had always felt that ankles were fairly safe parts of the female anatomy to look at, until now. Now, all he could think about was encircling one of those neat ankles with his fingers, trailing them up under all that satin until she uncrossed those legs and parted her thighs for him…

No. Hadn't he already decided he couldn't risk getting any closer to his wife until they agreed terms? He needed her tied to him for good before he risked anything—pregnancy or worse. He couldn't take the chance that he'd grow attached, start imagining their future together, if she might walk out on him at any moment. And he wasn't about to let brandy and satin derail the only part of his plan that was still intact.

'Did you want to talk about the marriage contract?' he asked, straightening himself in his chair and placing his full glass out of easy reach on the table. All he was feeling right now was lust. Nothing to worry about—as long as he didn't act on it. A one-night stand would be one thing, a temporary release—and wow, did he want that right now. But a man couldn't have a one-night stand with his own wife. That wasn't how this worked.

'Not exactly.' The smile she gave him now wasn't a memory at all. It was all new—teasing and tempting and tantalising. The sort of smile Flynn Ashton would never have been allowed to see if he hadn't married this woman that morning.

Suddenly, the whole fiasco seemed worthwhile, just for a glimpse of that smile. Even if he couldn't do anything about it—yet.

Yet. That was the key. He didn't need to close

this door forever, didn't need to shut down what this could be completely. He just needed to put it on ice until they got the details sorted. Who knew, the anticipation might even make the final outcome all the sweeter.

He just needed to exercise a little patience, that was all. And who knew patience better than him? The man who'd spent his life waiting to belong, for a place in the family, to be trusted with the business. He was so close now and he couldn't let his libido screw that up for him.

'I was thinking that there could be certain perks to this being married thing,' Helena went on, and Flynn focused very hard on not imagining those perks.

'I'm not sure—'

'I mean, we have this great opportunity to get to know each other better, for one thing.' Helena folded her legs up under her so she could lean over the arm of the chair, bringing her closer to him. He could smell her skin. She smelt like roses, and it was going to kill him.

'I've known you since you were born,' Flynn pointed out. 'I think we know each other pretty well.'

'Maybe.' Helena's answering smile was brief, and shaded. Almost sad. Flynn frowned; he'd known earlier, talking with her father, that he was missing something about Helena's past. That sad smile just made him want to know what even more. 'But we're different people now.'

'Than when we were children?' Flynn laughed, but he knew it sounded forced. 'I should hope so.'

'We're different people than we were this morning, Flynn,' Helena said, her beautiful face suddenly serious. 'You're a husband now, and I'm a wife. I'm Mrs Flynn Ashton now, remember?'

Sobered, Flynn nodded his agreement. 'I know. And that's…it's a big change for both of us. And that's why I think we need to spend some time figuring out what that means, for *our* futures, not just the family or the business.'

Helena blinked and sat back a little. 'I'm glad you feel that way.'

'What did you expect?' Flynn asked, not sure he wanted to hear the answer.

'Well, you disappeared from our wedding to hole up with my father and yours—presumably to discuss how our marriage impacts on the shareholders or something.' Helena shrugged. 'You can understand my belief that the human part of this marriage comes second.'

'It's not that,' Flynn assured her. 'But our parents are flying out tomorrow morning and I wanted to deal with them before they go. So that we don't have to think about them at all while we enjoy our honeymoon.' Instead, he could focus on getting Helena to sign the blasted marriage agreement so that when they got back to London he could put his energies into taking over as CEO of Morrison-Ashton, rather than firefighting whatever actions his father decided to take to solve the problem.

'Our honeymoon…' Helena's tongue darted out to lick her lips and Flynn's mind flew from business back to their first kiss. The way she'd melted against him, how his hands had clenched at her hips. How all he'd wanted in the world was to draw her closer and closer to him…

Not helping.

'I had some ideas about our honeymoon,' Helena went on. 'And getting to know each other better during it.' She leant in again and Flynn forced himself to pull back, to keep a distance between them, even if it was somehow actually physically painful.

'I had some thoughts too,' he said. 'I think the first thing we need to do is get the paperwork sorted.'

Helena blinked at him then shifted back, away. 'Paperwork.'

'I think it's important that we both know where we stand in this marriage.' He kept his gaze fixed on hers as he spoke. He wasn't hiding away from her, or pretending he didn't know what she was offering. But he needed to be plain about the way things were going to be.

No sex until they had the papers signed. Even if it felt as if it might kill him.

'You mean your father wants to make sure I've signed away my rights to anything worthwhile before I get my feminine claws into you.' Helena got to her feet, shaking her head. 'You know, he really doesn't have to worry. I don't want your money or your business. I don't even want this stupid ring, but I can't get it off my fat finger.' She waved her left hand in front of his face and Flynn reached out to grab it.

'You agreed to this marriage.' He ran his finger over the band, soothing the red skin there, and after a moment she stopped trying to pull it away again. Progress. 'You even pushed this ring into place. Nobody forced you into anything, and the only thing you signed before we said our vows was a meaningless invitation.'

'I know that.' She sounded irritable now. Flynn never imagined that could be a step up from seductive but, under the circumstances, he was happy to go with it. 'And I know we need the paperwork so that we can get out of this whole mess neatly when the time comes—'

'That's not why.' They were married now. It was time to disabuse her of any notion that this marriage was a temporary thing for him. 'We need it so that you can be my wife, completely, without any of this confusion or people talking about us. We need it to make us official. Legitimate.'

Helena's eyes narrowed and she pulled her hand from his, but he could still feel the phantom memory of the cool metal of her ring against his fingertips.

'You mean to make you legitimate,' she said, her glare accusing. 'You need the paperwork to prove you're really part of the family. You think it'll make it easier for you as CEO when your dad steps down, now Zeke's gone.'

'That's part of it,' Flynn allowed. 'But not all.'

Helena stood, shifting so her weight was on one leg and her hip cocked out for her hand to rest on it. It emphasised the curve of her waist in a way Flynn really shouldn't be thinking about right now, and he tried to focus on the unhappy curl of her lips rather than anything below them.

'Really?' she asked, sounding unconvinced. 'Then tell me this. If you'd married Thea today, would you be down here drinking brandy alone? Or would you be in bed with her right now?'

CHAPTER FIVE

HELENA ALMOST DIDN'T want to hear the answer. It was a stupid question—one that neither of them could escape from now it'd been asked. Maybe that was for the best. If things had gone to plan, Flynn would have married her sister today. She knew that Thea hadn't loved him, but she'd never really given much thought to how Flynn felt about Thea. She'd just assumed, given his usual pragmatic, spreadsheet-based approach to the whole thing, that it was a business convenience.

She'd even wondered idly once or twice if Flynn was gay and his marriage to Thea an elaborate cover to hide the truth from Ezekiel. Heaven knew the old man was hidebound and rigid about everything else. No reason to assume that he'd deal with a son who liked men any better than he'd dealt with a son who ran out and abandoned the family business like Zeke had.

Flynn wasn't gay. No gay guy could have kissed her the way he had at the reception. And, besides, she knew when a guy wanted her—and

Flynn's eyes when she'd walked in had spoken volumes. Lusty volumes of erotic poetry.

He wanted her. But he wasn't going to take her, even offered up on a plate. In Helena's experience, there were limited reasons for that sort of restraint—and they usually came down to being faithful to someone else.

What if Flynn had really loved Thea? What if he was heartbroken right now, drowning his sorrows in brandy while she swanned in wearing white satin and tried to seduce him?

Could she have made a bigger mess of this? But there was no going back now. She needed to know the truth.

'Tell me honestly, Flynn. Would you have slept with Thea tonight?' she asked again, and Flynn's gaze slipped away from hers.

'Probably.' His shoulders lifted slightly then slumped. 'We'd talked about…well…getting to know each other as man and wife, from the start.'

Helena's jaw tightened. She could almost imagine the conversation, probably squeezed in between a meeting about the quarterly projections and a client presentation. Thea, cool and calm and business-like, the way she only ever was when she was working, not dating. Flynn, as unflappable as ever, giving equal gravity to the budget and his sex life.

One of them had probably even said the words:

in the interest of mutual satisfaction or something.

'But it was different with Thea,' Flynn said, a hint of apology in his voice. 'We were…well, I was…'

In love, Helena finished for him in her head. And that was something Helena couldn't match up to. She'd thought she could be enough for him, for now. But not if he was in love with her sister.

Flynn sighed. 'We had paperwork,' he said in the end, as if that explained everything.

For Flynn, it probably did.

'That's all you want from this marriage? Paperwork?' Helena gripped the back of the chair she stood behind, keeping it between them like a shield. A screen, at least. How humiliating to be having this conversation in almost see-through nightwear. How had this ever seemed like a good idea?

'No.' That was his firm voice. His don't-mess-with-me business voice. She'd heard of it, mostly from Thea, but he'd never used it on her before. They'd never been close enough for him to have the opportunity, not since she was fifteen.

'Then what *do* you want?' She didn't care if she was pleading. She needed to make sense of this if she hoped to have any chance of sleeping tonight. She swept a hand down the side of her negligee. 'You don't want this. You don't want happily ever after. But you don't seem to want a quickie divorce either. Whatever happens next, we're stuck with each other for at least the next two weeks. So tell me—what is it you *do* want?'

'I want a wife. I want paperwork. I want something to follow the plan just *once*.' He grabbed his glass and downed the remaining brandy. Helena just stared at him. Was that Flynn losing his temper? she wondered. She'd never seen it before. And still, it seemed so…insubstantial.

'I'm sorry,' he said, as if he'd thrown the glass at her or something. 'It's just…it's been a long day, and not one bit of it has gone the way I expected. I'm still…adjusting.'

To being married to the wrong woman. To losing the woman he'd actually *wanted* to marry. She couldn't even blame him.

'Right,' she said, as if her life hadn't been turned upside down a couple of times in the last twenty-four hours, too. 'I can understand that.'

Flynn looked up, his eyes red and tired. 'For you too, I know. It's been…'

'One hell of a day.'

'Yeah.' They stared at each other for a long moment, and Helena felt the knowledge that she was tied to this man, for better or for worse, sinking into her bones in a way it never had when she'd said the words.

This was her future, whatever happened next.

He'd always be her husband, even if he became an ex. They were joined—and she didn't understand the first thing about him.

This Flynn, the one she'd seen tonight, was nothing like the one her fourteen-year-old self had thought herself in love with. He wasn't kind, noble and knowing. He wasn't even the unfeeling, emotionally detached man she'd assumed he had to be to deal with his fiancée running out on him. This Flynn cared. He felt. He hurt.

And this was the man she'd married. The man she intended to keep secrets from until they could *un*marry.

'I should...' She wiggled her fingers towards the door. 'Sleep would probably help. Both of us.'

'Yeah.' Flynn sighed. 'I'll head up in a moment, too. I just have one phone call to make.'

'Now? It's two in the morning, Flynn.'

'I know. But this can't wait.'

'I'll never understand that,' she admitted. 'You and your dad—and Thea. The way you're married to the business. I mean...' She winced as she realised what she'd said.

But it didn't seem to register with Flynn. 'This isn't business.'

Not business? Then who would take his call at two a.m.? Unless...was he phoning Thea? She didn't want to know if he was.

Helena turned to leave, but paused in the doorway as she remembered her original plan for their sleeping arrangements—before the negligee and the discovery that her husband might well be in love with her sister, even now.

'I thought…maybe it would be a good idea for you to sleep in my old room? Tonight, at least. I had the maid move your things. It's right next to the bridal suite, so it makes it a little less likely for you to be caught out on the other side of the building in the morning, when you're supposed to be ravishing your new wife.'

He actually flinched at the words and Helena swallowed down the spike of pain she felt at that. No, she definitely wasn't enough for Flynn Ashton, even after everything she'd done today.

'Okay. I'll do that then. I'll see you in the morning, Helena.' He said it kindly, a sop to her poor hopeful ideas of a night with her husband.

'Yeah. In the morning.'

Maybe things would look brighter with the sunrise. They sure couldn't look much darker.

Flynn didn't sleep much.

He'd woken his solicitor up the moment Helena left and asked him to book a flight over to discuss the new marriage contract. Explaining why that was necessary hadn't been fun, and he rather suspected he'd have to do it again in the morning anyway, once Henry was properly awake. Even the best contract solicitor in London needed a little time to surface from sleep before his brilliance began to shine.

That vital task performed, he'd headed up to bed, pausing at the top of the stairs while he considered his options. Helena had a point; sleeping in her old room would make the chance of discovery in the morning less likely. And since apparently his stuff was already there anyway, he'd trudged off in the direction of the bridal suite, letting himself into the room next door. And if his body tugged him towards another door, another bed, another body, well, he resisted. Just.

But lying in sheets that still smelled of her perfume, of roses, of her skin, made it impossible not to think of Helena. His wife.

He'd hurt her tonight, he'd seen it in her eyes, even if he wasn't sure exactly what he'd said wrong. Everything, probably. He was out of practice at dealing with women. For the past few years, it had only been Thea for him, and that wasn't exactly a normal relationship. One of the most reassuring parts of it was being able to discuss things openly and clearly, without misunderstandings.

But with Helena…they didn't have that grounding. And so he'd miscalculated and caused her pain. So now he needed to try and find a way to fix that and make sure it didn't happen again.

Henry's arrival should solve the second part of that. Once they had their expectations down on paper, things would get easier between them. But making things up to her…that was all on him.

Flynn eventually drifted off thinking of ways to improve relations with his wife, only to be awoken by his internal clock a mere three hours later. Six a.m. on the dot; he knew without checking his phone. It always was. He'd been waking up at six for so long now he couldn't sleep in if he wanted to.

Actually, today he wanted to. If he could sleep, he would miss the departing parents and family. Helena could get over last night with coffee and breakfast, and by the time he finally emerged the world would be stable and right again.

Flynn sighed, rolled out of bed and headed for the shower. Heat and steam were the next best thing to sleep, anyway.

Clean and awake, Flynn towelled off and reached for his usual suit before remembering that he was on holiday. More than that, he was on his *honeymoon*. It might not resemble what other people expected from a honeymoon, but it was the best he was going to get. And he certainly wasn't going to wear a suit for it.

Even if he suspected that today, his first day of marriage, would look very similar to every other day that had come before it. He had work to do, as ever. And he had to review the marriage agreement he'd had with Thea before Henry arrived.

But first he had to make sure his parents actually left for London. At least, with them gone, he wouldn't have to worry about Ezekiel meddling or Isabella upsetting Helena.

Of course, with the departure of everyone else, it would just be him and Helena left together. Alone.

And that, Flynn decided, could get very interesting indeed. At the very least, it would give him a solid chance to make things up to his new wife.

All the more reason to make sure that Henry got there soon.

Helena woke the morning after her wedding, just as she'd gone to bed: alone. Why on earth did that feel like a surprise? she wondered as she lay back on the luxurious sheets and stared at the ceiling.

Here she was, the first day of her honeymoon, and she wasn't sure she was going to see her husband at all. Wasn't sure that she wanted to either.

Except their parents were leaving that morning. He'd have to be there to see them off, right?

And if Flynn was there, did she really have to be there too?

Helena sighed. Sadly, yes, she did. This was the first full day of the charade that was set to take over her life for the next however long—the act of being a devoted and dutiful wife. At least, with the remaining guests and family gone, the only people she'd have to keep it up for were the villa staff—until they got home to London, anyway.

Dragging herself out of bed, she showered and dressed quickly before heading down to the entrance hall, her still damp hair curling around her shoulders.

'The car for the airport is here,' Flynn said, walking in through the front door just as she came down the stairs.

'Unlike the people it's here to transport.' Helena looked pointedly around the empty hallway, trying to ignore the way her heart jumped, just a little, at the sight of him. Could she be more pathetic? He might have married her, but he'd made it very clear that all he wanted was the paperwork.

They stared at each other for a long moment and Helena felt the cool stone walls pressing in as the silence between them grew. She'd never had a problem finding things to talk to Flynn— or anyone else—about before, but all of a sudden it was as if the rings they wore had sucked all the small talk out of them.

We're good at this, she reminded herself desperately. *We're the ones who keep the conver-*

sation going, who smooth over the awkward silences and the embarrassing comments!

But apparently that skill only worked with people they weren't married to. Or when one of them hadn't turned down a wedding night in the marital bed, at least. Great.

'Maybe I should go and check on them,' Flynn said eventually, moving towards the stairs. Helena tried to dodge out of his way, but miscalculated, her foot slipping on the bottom few steps.

She reached for the banister but Flynn was there first, grabbing her around the waist with both arms to keep her upright.

Helena waited for her heartbeat to return to normal speed now she was safe. It didn't.

Looking up, she saw honest concern in Flynn's golden caramel eyes. His very close eyes. Not far from his very close lips. So close, in fact, that she'd only have to move a centimetre or two and they'd be kissing. Like they'd done after the speeches. And that kiss had hinted at so much more…

Until he'd turned down her advances just a few hours later. The memory of his dismissal settled over her like a cold shower.

'Just look at you two lovebirds! *Such* a beautiful sight.' Isabella's voice rang out across the hallway, echoing off the stone walls as she descended the stairs. Flynn pulled away so quickly that Helena ended up grabbing the banister anyway. *So much for chivalry.*

'Let me help you with that, Mother.' Flynn jogged up the stairs to take his mother's suitcase from her and carried it down. 'Where are Dad and Thomas?'

Isabella rolled her eyes. 'In the study, I believe. Last-minute business meeting before our flight.'

Helena saw the look of irritation that crossed Flynn's face, but Isabella either missed or chose to ignore it. Feeling left out, was he? She supposed she'd better prepare herself for two weeks of him sloping off to check his email and taking business calls during lunch.

That was if they spent any time together at all. What if he just intended to work all through the honeymoon?

Helena shook away the thought. She had to look on the bright side or she was going to go mad. So what if her husband had better things to do on their honeymoon than spend time with her? That just gave her more opportunities to go exploring, to see more of the country, maybe go back to that pretty jewellery shop she'd found with Thea in the nearest town. She could treat herself to something pretty then have lunch in that little *trattoria*. Maybe flirt with a nice Italian man… The thought stopped abruptly.

She couldn't do that any more, could she? Not

now she was married. And especially not once she signed Flynn's blasted paperwork with its ironclad fidelity clause. Not that she had any particular plans to go out and pick up a guy or anything. It wasn't really her style, was it? But she did *like* men, had several close male friends and enjoyed the warm buzz she got from flirting with them, just a little, even knowing that they would never do anything about it.

But that was off the table now. Flynn would probably have private detectives following her around, photographing her having lunch and researching every man she ever spoke to. And if he didn't, his father certainly would.

Yeah, she really hadn't thought this whole thing through.

A door opened just down the corridor and she heard her father's laugh as he and Ezekiel emerged from their conference, dragging their cases behind them.

'All ready?' Flynn asked the men. 'The car for the airport is here.'

Ezekiel nodded and one of the villa staff darted forward to take their cases out to the car. Flynn followed with Isabella's. Helena stood awkwardly, waiting for whatever happened next. The moment they left, everything would change again and she was beginning to fear that her bright attitude wasn't going to last a full two weeks.

'Well, have a good journey home, all of you,' she said. 'And we'll see you in London in a fortnight, I guess.'

Isabella nodded and leant in to kiss the air beside Helena's cheeks. 'We'll have the house all ready for you both. Then you and I can sit down and discuss your social calendar.'

Social calendar? 'Great.'

Ezekiel nodded his own farewell then walked out of the front door with his wife, leaving Helena alone with Thomas.

'You've got two weeks here, Helena,' he said, studying her face with serious eyes. Helena's breath caught in her throat. She and Thea had always known that their father was easy-going and affable—but only to a point. When he turned serious, they knew it really mattered. 'Use them wisely. You've made your choice and you need to stick with it now. So make this work.'

He didn't really need to add the *or else*, Helena supposed. She knew well enough what happened when she disappointed her father.

'And if you speak to your sister,' he added, pausing by the door, 'tell her we need to discuss her future. Sooner rather than later.'

Helena nodded stiffly. She didn't envy her sister that conversation.

But then, Thea probably wouldn't envy Helena two weeks in Tuscany trying to 'make things work' with a husband who didn't want her, either.

Well, if all Flynn wanted was a paperwork wife, Helena could give him that. Watching as he waved to their parents' departing car from the front step, Helena made a decision. If this was all business anyway, she'd let Flynn get on with his—while she focused on her own life. She'd cleared her calendar for the month around the wedding, knowing things would be manic enough without adding any new projects for her burgeoning interior design business into the mix. But here she was with time on her hands, her laptop and freakishly fast Internet access, given their location. It was the perfect chance to get on with the new website she'd been planning for months.

Time for her to get on with her own future for a while.

Their married life had slipped into a routine surprisingly quickly, Flynn realised a few days later. Every morning he woke, went for a run, returned to the villa to shower and dress, then sat down for breakfast. Helena usually joined him then and they made polite, if sparse, conversation over the English papers he'd arranged to have delivered.

Then Flynn would settle into his father's study to work while Helena did…whatever it was she did all day. Sometimes they'd see each other for lunch, sometimes not. Dinner they usually took together in the dining room, and Helena always turned in for bed first.

There had been no repeat of her wedding night offer, something for which Flynn was profoundly grateful as Henry had been held up in London and wasn't able to get out to Tuscany until the end of the week. As much as he wanted the paperwork sorted before he allowed himself to really invest in the marriage, he knew his own limitations. No man had willpower strong enough to resist Helena in that negligee night upon night, whatever the stakes.

Still, he thought as he took his morning run on the fourth day, he didn't want the distance between them to grow so much as to be insurmountable, either. Once Henry arrived he needed Helena on side, ready to work with him, ready to make this marriage real.

With an extra burst of energy he took the last stretch up the drive to the villa at a sprint, the thought of a calendar entry he'd barely registered the day before spurring him on.

Back in his room, he checked his phone as he caught his breath again. He smiled. Right there, scheduled neatly in his personal calendar by his PA, who'd been put in charge of all the honeymoon plans, was exactly the right way to make things up to Helena. A romantic tour of a Tuscan vineyard, complete with wine-tasting, lunch and perhaps a drive through the countryside. Perfect for the honeymooning couple.

It would mean taking the whole day off to do it properly. If he'd been with Thea, as planned, they'd have spent half a day there then both headed home to catch up with emails, he imagined. But Helena, he suspected, required a different hand. After four days of distance, this needed to be all or nothing.

And Flynn was going all in.

Helena ignored the first three knocks on her door. She'd stayed up late after dinner working again on the new website and had planned to catch up on her sleep with a well-earned lie-in—especially as it meant she stood a better chance of avoiding her husband at breakfast. The endless awkward pauses and stilted conversations over the dining tables were becoming more than she could bear. Would it be like this in London? She hoped not.

But the fourth knock she couldn't ignore, especially as the door opened seconds after it.

'Helena…you're not up?' Flynn closed the door behind him and stared at her, a frown line deepening between his eyebrows.

'It's only nine-thirty.' Helena shuffled into a sitting position, glad that she'd slept in her comfortable shorts and T-shirt instead of the ridiculous negligee. 'We're supposed to be on our honeymoon. I'm maintaining the happy couple illusion.'

'The car's picking us up in half an hour. You might want to get up.' Flynn crossed to the bathroom while Helena just blinked at him in confusion. 'I'll get the shower running. Give it a chance to warm up for you.'

'I can run my own shower,' Helena protested, swinging her legs over the side of the bed. Apparently she was getting up. 'And, anyway, what car?'

She heard the sound of water running and Flynn re-emerged. 'The car to take us on our vineyard trip. Didn't it get put on your calendar? I've got it all arranged for us.'

Helena felt that same chill that had overtaken her on her wedding night begin to snake its way through her veins, despite the steam from the shower seeping into the room and the warm summer morning outside.

'You mean you had it all arranged for you and Thea.' She was not jealous of her sister, Helena reminded herself. It wasn't as if she was in love with Flynn either. She just liked to know where she stood, that was all.

'I arranged it for my wife and me. That's you, in case you'd forgotten.'

'Not likely,' Helena muttered.

Flynn headed back towards the door. 'Car will be here at ten. I'll meet you in the foyer.'

And then Helena was alone again, with only the sound of falling water to keep her company.

A vineyard tour. Presumably that included wine-tasting, so things could be worse. Maybe there'd even be lunch. Taking a deep breath, Helena decided to focus on the positive. Paying attention to the good things in life, she'd found, was sometimes the only way to avoid drowning in the despair of all the bad things.

So—good things only.

The sun was shining, the new website was going well enough that she'd earned a break, and she would have wine and food in the sunshine today. Maybe she could even talk the maid into coffee and something resembling breakfast before they left, if she was quick.

Lots of good things to distract from the one awful thing. It was going to be a good day.

Forcing a smile, she hopped in the shower, washing away her bad mood with the soap suds. By the time she emerged again, the maid had left coffee and a pastry on the chest of drawers and Helena sipped and nibbled happily as she flicked through her wardrobe to find something suitable for a newly married woman on her honeymoon, taking a tour with her husband.

She really hadn't packed for this. Mostly, she'd

just been working in shorts and a T-shirt so far. But today's trip seemed important to Flynn, so she guessed it should be important to her, too. Maybe they'd even manage to learn how to speak to each other again. That kind of milestone required more than a pair of shorts, Helena decided.

In the end, she settled on a sunny yellow cotton dress, patterned with daisies around the hem, and slipped her feet into white sandals. She twisted her wet hair into a knot at the back of her head, knowing it would dry quickly enough in the sun and give her pretty waves when she let it down that evening. Even with ten minutes to add sun protection and a little light make-up, she was still ready well before ten.

Grabbing her straw hat and bag, she headed down the stairs to find Flynn already in the entrance hall.

'You were quick,' Flynn said with a smile. 'I thought I'd be waiting a while for you.'

'Shows how little you know me.' Helena arched her eyebrows. 'I'm very efficient—when I want to be.'

'Well, thank you for your efficiency.' He glanced away for a moment before meeting her gaze again. 'I'm sorry we haven't had much time to spend together so far this week. With Zeke's surprise coup, getting Dad to make me CEO, things are frantic at work, making sure everything's in place.'

'I understand,' Helena said as coolly as she could. 'I had work to do too, anyway.'

Flynn blinked and Helena realised he probably hadn't even known she had a job, beyond helping out with his wedding. Irritation rose in her chest. Rosebud Interiors might not be much compared to the might of Morrison-Ashton, but it was still her company.

'That's good, then,' he said. 'Maybe you can tell me more about it over lunch?'

Some of the irritation faded away when she realised he did sound honestly interested. 'Yeah, okay.'

'Great. Well, then, let's get going.' Flynn held out an arm for her. After a moment she took it and was rewarded by a warm private smile. 'I'm looking forward to a day out with my wife.'

Helena beamed back, an unexpected warmth blossoming inside her despite herself at the words 'my wife'. Maybe this day wouldn't be *all* bad.

CHAPTER SIX

As THE CAR flew through the Tuscan countryside, Flynn settled back into his seat and ran through his plan for the day again in his head.

Main objective: to make Helena comfortable with this marriage in time for Henry's arrival. Or was the main objective to get Helena to sit down and sensibly discuss the marriage contract? One led to the other, admittedly, but a firm objective was the first step of any plan. So, which was it?

Maybe he needed a broader plan. Make the objective a signed contract before they headed back to London. In which case, today's steps broke down into—

'Oh, wow!' Helena wound down her window and stuck her head half outside the car. 'Look at this place, Flynn!'

Resisting the urge to pull her back inside, where a passing car was less likely to lop her head off, Flynn tried to look around her at what had made her so excited. Whatever it was, it fitted nicely with his plan, at least. Coaxing Helena into a better mood was definitely step one.

Outside, field after field of grapevines sunned themselves as they ripened and, up ahead, Flynn could see the farmhouse from the photo his PA had attached to the diary entry. This was the right place then, at least.

'It's gorgeous.' Helena ducked back into the car, her smile far more authentic this time. 'This is where we're doing the tasting?' she asked as the driver took another twist in the rough driveway at considerable speed.

'This is the place.' Flynn made a mental note about a raise for his PA as he pulled out his phone and checked the notes on the diary entry again. 'A tour of the vineyards, followed by a tasting with antipasti, then a drive to a nearby *taverna* for lunch, where I believe they serve the wine from the estate.'

'Sounds perfect.' She flashed him a quick grin that showed her neat white teeth. 'Very romantic.'

'I think that was the plan.' He tucked his phone back in his pocket as the car reached the top of the drive and slowed to a stop. 'At least, that's what I asked my PA to organise.'

'You asked her to organise romance?' Helena asked, eyebrows raised. 'Isn't that a little counter-intuitive?'

'I don't see why.' The driver opened Helena's door, so Flynn opened his own and stepped out into the late morning sun. 'Most things can be improved by a little planning.'

'Still…romance needs a certain sort of spontaneity. Don't you think?'

She really wasn't anything like her sister, Flynn mused. Although, given Thea's own last-minute change of plan for love, perhaps they had more in common than he'd imagined.

'I think that people like to think that the good things in life are natural, that they just happen,' he said. 'But in my experience a lack of planning tends to lead to unfortunate outcomes rather than good ones.'

Helena stared at him over the bonnet of the car. 'Boy, have you been having the wrong experiences.'

Maybe she was right. But not about the planning. And if they wanted to get along equably enough as man and wife… Mentally, Flynn added: *Convince Helena of the merits of forward planning* to his schedule for the day.

He had always liked a challenge.

'Mr and Mrs Ashton! Welcome. I'm Gia.' The dark-haired woman stepped forward on to the driveway and shook Helena's hand enthusiastically before moving on to Flynn.

'Call me Flynn,' he said, taking her hand in both of his. Her husband looked far more relaxed in the company of this stranger than he did in hers, Helena thought.

'And I'm Helena,' she added with a little wave. 'So...is this your home?'

Gia laughed, a low, mellow sound. 'It is! It belonged to my great-grandparents, then my grandparents, then my parents. And when they retired three years ago I took it over with my husband.'

'And began producing some of the most renowned Chianti in the region,' Flynn said. Gia's gaze moved to him, her eyebrows raised. Helena would have done the same, were it not Flynn the Planner talking. 'I read the website in the car,' he added with a shrug.

'It's good to have a truly interested visitor,' Gia said. 'Now, why don't you come inside with me and have a coffee before we start our tour?'

'That sounds like a fantastic idea,' Helena agreed, even as she saw Flynn check his watch. Good grief, the man was going to have to learn to find flex in his schedule to allow for coffee or they were never going to make it through the fortnight without killing each other.

The coffee was dark and rich, the farmhouse kitchen shady and cool—both a welcome respite after the air-conditioned swerving of the car. Helena felt her stomach settle and her shoulders relax as she sat and peppered Gia with questions about the house and the vineyard.

'I was working in America—California, in fact—until five years ago,' Gia said, pushing a plate of *biscotti* towards Helena.

'Making wine?' Helena asked, helping herself.

Gia shook her head. 'Real estate, believe it or not. But I toured plenty of the vineyards out there with clients. But then one year I came home for Christmas and, over dinner, my parents told me it was time for them to retire. They didn't want to interrupt my career, so they were planning to sell the vineyard.' She gave a small shrug and reached for a *biscotti*. 'I couldn't let them do it.'

'So you took it on yourself instead,' Flynn said. 'Very brave.'

Gia gave him a lopsided smile. 'I don't think I realised the risk I was taking until later. I came here with no plan, no real training, no idea what I was doing. But I learned fast and I studied hard. I took courses, asked questions and paid attention to *everything*. My parents stayed on to help for the first year or so, then I met my husband and he came on board, and between us all we found a way to make it work.'

Helena raised her eyebrows at Flynn across the table, sipping at her coffee while she waited for him to notice. Even he had to acknowledge everything Gia had built here without a plan.

But Flynn merely raised a single eyebrow in return then turned his attention back to Gia. 'I imagine you needed to work up a business plan and so forth once you took it over?'

'Of course. But that initial decision—that first jump. I never for a moment planned that, until that Christmas Day when I suddenly couldn't imagine doing anything else.'

Like her, on the morning of their wedding, Helena realised. She'd never really, truly imagined stepping into Thea's place if she decided not to go through with the marriage. But once she'd left, and she'd seen Flynn standing there...she couldn't imagine not marrying him in her place. Even though it was utterly, utterly crazy and unplanned.

Of course, Flynn would probably argue that marrying Helena was the closest thing to following his plan that he could manage on short notice.

Not exactly romantic.

'Come on,' Gia said, jumping to her feet. 'If you've finished your coffee, let's take a look around the vineyard.'

Helena gulped down the last mouthful of her coffee, grabbed another *biscotti* for the road and followed their guide out of the back door. She had a feeling that Gia was a woman who would appreciate the spontaneous aspect of romance. And she had an idea Gia might be able to help her with—if she could get her alone for a moment.

* * *

Flynn watched Helena as she skipped between the vines, peppering Gia with questions at every step. Gia, for her part, answered every one thoughtfully, following Helena at a more careful pace. Eventually Flynn tuned out of what they were saying altogether and just studied his wife.

She was golden in the sunlight, shining with—no, radiating—life and energy. Now they had escaped the villa, she seemed to have come to life. She'd been lovely in her borrowed wedding dress, gorgeous in that slippery silky thing on their wedding night, and pretty in the simple tailored shorts and tees she'd been wearing around the villa—but today, in a simple sundress and sandals, she was beautiful. She was *alive*.

Absently, Flynn pulled his phone from his pocket to check if Henry had sent through his flight details yet. The sooner they got this contract sorted, the sooner he could start making this marriage everything he'd planned for it to be. But there were no messages from his solicitor, or his PA, and as Flynn frowned at the screen Helena turned around to scowl at him.

'No working on honeymoon,' she said, plucking the phone from his hand and dropping it into her ridiculously large straw bag.

Gia's face tensed behind Helena. Flynn suspected she'd seen this between guests before, and that it didn't always end well. Except he and Helena weren't most guests, were they?

'I hope you can find that again in there,' he said mildly. 'It's got all the rest of our honeymoon activities scheduled on it.'

'All of them?' Helena asked with arched brows, and Gia laughed.

'Perhaps not all,' Flynn allowed.

'Good.' Helena twirled back to face Gia. 'Because I might have one or two surprises to add to it.'

Flynn's body tightened, just a little, at the warmth and promise in her voice that had been so absent the last few days, and he took a moment before following the women along the path. Maybe he'd plan a few surprises for Helena, too. The moment he had that contract signed.

Gia ended their tour right back where they had begun—at the back door to the farmhouse. Flynn wasn't sure if he'd learned very much about growing grapevines, but he was certainly ready for the wine-tasting.

As Gia opened the door to let them back into the kitchen, a man's voice floated out over a babble of childish nonsense. 'Trust me, *baba*, you won't like that one.'

'Is he after the salami or the wine today?' Laughing, Gia crossed the kitchen to give both man and baby a kiss on the cheek. 'Helena, Flynn. This is my husband, Roberto, and our son, Casper.'

'Pleased to meet you,' Flynn said, glancing over at Helena. She stood, mesmerised by the child, her lower lip trapped between her teeth. Was she thinking of the child they might have soon? He hoped so. 'I'm Flynn Ashton, and this is my wife, Helena.'

Breaking her reverie, Helena smiled suddenly and waved at Casper. 'Hi.'

'We'll get out of your way now,' Roberto said. 'Everything should be set out. We'd have left already if somebody hadn't got a little hungry.' He held up a small bowl with some fresh fruit cut into baby-sized pieces. 'Come on, Casper. Let's see what birds we can spot from the terrace today.'

As Roberto and the baby wandered back out again, Gia watched them go. They were a nice family, Flynn thought. Obviously working together to keep everything—childcare and wine-making—running smoothly. He admired that.

He wanted that for himself. He'd discussed it with Thea, of course, although he'd planned to do so in greater detail after the wedding. He didn't want a wife waiting at home for him, organising parties and social events while sending her children off to boarding school, the way Isabella had done. He wanted a family where every member belonged and felt at home.

Watching Helena in the sunlight, he'd almost been able to picture it—more so even than he'd ever managed with Thea. It was possible, he thought with a smile, that losing his fiancée on his wedding day might turn out to be the best possible thing for his future. Whatever Helena said about their union being temporary, if they wanted, her behaviour said otherwise. If she didn't intend for it to last, why would she have accosted him in that negligee on their wedding night? No, Helena wanted this to work as much as he did—seeing her staring at the baby only confirmed that for him.

They'd talk, just as he planned. Maybe over lunch. Once she understood what this marriage meant to him, the contract negotiations were bound to go more smoothly. And then they could get on with properly enjoying the honeymoon.

He smiled again at the thought, before realising that Helena had already sat down at the tasting table and Gia was pouring their first wines. He slipped into the seat beside his wife and thought, just for a moment, about taking her hand.

But when he looked across, he saw a frown line marring her forehead and realised that the sunny, happy, teasing Helena he'd admired outside had gone—and he had no idea what had changed.

But he planned to find out.

Helena barely remembered anything from their tasting, later. She hoped she'd nodded in the right places, and said the right things, but she had no real idea. Flynn hadn't said anything, so perhaps she'd managed to keep up the show. To pretend that everything was fine and normal. That seeing Casper hadn't sent her mind spiralling back eight years.

Normally she was better at this—at being around babies and children. But today, with Flynn there beside her, a hopeful look in his eyes…all she'd been able to think about was the baby girl she'd given away.

Eventually, Flynn checked his watch and gave Gia an apologetic smile. 'This has been absolutely fascinating. Thank you so much for taking the time to show us around, and letting us taste your wonderful wines.'

'It's been my pleasure,' Gia said, beaming.

Roberto and Casper came out to wave them off and Helena tried to ignore the tug that still pulled at her middle, even after all these years. Instead, she plastered on a smile as she waved back then got into the car.

As the driver pulled away from the farmhouse,

Helena handed Flynn back his phone, tipped her head back against the headrest and closed her eyes. But her mind still filled with babies.

Casper was a beautiful child, she thought, remembering his pudgy fingers clenched around a piece of apple, and his big brown eyes under dark curls. Nothing at all like the girl she'd given away eight long years ago, with her fine, pale baby down on her head and her unfocused blue eyes. There was no reason for him to remind Helena of her own child, except that every baby she saw did.

Probably always would, she'd realised by now.

But the life her daughter lived…she hoped that was like Casper's. Happy and full of family and laughter in a way it never could have been if Helena had kept her.

She'd done the right thing, however much it hurt. And sometimes that was all she could cling on to.

Squeezing her eyes tighter for a moment, willing away any tears, any signs of weakness, Helena tucked away all those feelings, all the regrets and what-ifs that rose up when she least wanted them, and returned to the present day. To her husband. Blinking a few times, she watched the Tuscan countryside flashing past the car window, all greens and reds and yellows and bright, bright blues.

How could she be sad when the world around her was so beautiful?

Composed again, she twisted in her seat to look at Flynn. He was engrossed in his phone screen so she gave it a few moments before clearing her throat. Still nothing.

'Where are we going for lunch?' she asked.

'Hmm?' Flynn's head moved as if he were paying her his full attention, but his gaze remained attached to the screen in front of him. Helena almost laughed, but decided not to encourage him.

Instead, she snatched the phone from his hand again and selected his calendar app. 'Let's see...'

Flynn's fingers closed over the screen, warm against her own hand. 'I thought you wanted spontaneity and surprises with your romance.'

'Not when you already planned it. Or your PA did.'

'It's a surprise to both of us that way,' Flynn pointed out.

Helena rolled her eyes. 'I really don't think you understand spontaneity.'

'It doesn't matter now anyway,' Flynn said, taking the phone from her and tucking it in his top pocket as the car slowed to a stop. 'We're here.'

She'd known she wasn't getting that phone back.

The driver opened her car door and Helena

stepped out into the sunshine again, her head a little heavy from the drive and the wine-tasting. The *trattoria* they'd arrived at looked almost like someone's house, with its beautiful window boxes overflowing with flowers and the painted shutters thrown open. Helena spun slowly around to take in the view; nothing but fields and sunshine for miles, and the glint of a village a few miles down the road.

'You like it?' Flynn asked. He'd put on his sunglasses and Helena wished she could see his eyes. Surely even he had to admire the romance of a place like this.

'It's beautiful.' This was the sort of place she could imagine living—or at least designing. Nothing quite as grand as the villa they'd borrowed for the wedding, but cosy and homely and filled with good food and red flowers. It wasn't just beautiful; it was perfect.

'Then let's go in.' Flynn held his hand out to her and, after staring at it for a moment, Helena took it. She couldn't help but wonder, though, if it was a planned or spontaneous gesture. Either way, his hand felt warm and right in hers, so she decided not to ask.

Inside, parts of the restaurant's stone walls had been left bare, while others had been plastered and painted a creamy white that reflected the sunlight. Helena smiled at the happy mix of rustic and modern, finished with bright blooms in hand-blown glass vases, crisp table linen and an oversized clock hanging over the stone fireplace.

It was almost exactly how she'd have chosen to decorate it, given the chance.

They were shown to their table by an olive-skinned Italian girl in a neat black and white uniform. It wasn't a huge place—the ground floor had been mostly knocked through to make a large dining area, with the kitchen added on at the back of the house, as far as Helena could tell. Still, the fact that almost every other table was already occupied, considering such an out of the way location, gave Helena great hopes for the quality of the food. Despite the bread and antipasti she'd enjoyed at Gia's vineyard, her stomach started to rumble.

'What are you in the mood for?' Flynn asked as Helena cracked open the menu.

'Everything,' she answered, feasting on the lists of dishes printed on creamy paper in front of her. There was just the right amount of choice, she decided. Not too much, or it became impossible to decide, but enough that she felt she could consider each dish individually before picking her absolute favourite.

Flynn laughed. 'You like food, don't you?'

'Who doesn't?' The only question was: did she feel in the mood for meat or fish? And should they have a separate pasta course or just starters and mains? She reached for an olive from the bowl on the table between them to help her think. 'Everyone needs to eat.'

'Yes, but for some people it's just fuel. You really enjoy it.'

Helena glanced up to find his gaze settled on her, as if she were something to be studied, catalogued and understood. It was unnerving. But then, didn't she want to do the same to him? Understand where he came from, and where they were going? Maybe Flynn's thoughts had followed a similar thread, in which case the rest of the meal might go easier than she'd expected.

Closing the menu—she was settled on the *porcetta* anyway—Helena returned Flynn's interested gaze.

'What about you?' she asked. 'Do you cook? Or do you survive on takeaway Chinese like Thea when she's working?'

'I cook.' Flynn settled back in his chair. He hadn't even looked at the menu, she realised. 'Not often, but I can when the mood strikes me. I like eating fresh.'

'Me too. Fresh and in season always tastes better than pre-packaged.' She flashed him a grin. 'So, we do have some things in common, then. That's good.'

'It is,' Flynn agreed. 'But really, given our families, I never doubted we'd find some common ground.'

Helena gave a slight shrug. 'I don't know. I never really felt like a typical Morrison, not like Thea. I mean, I didn't go into the family business or anything.'

'No, but you grew up with the same expectations and weight of that family name,' Flynn said, more insightfully than she'd expected.

'And you grew up with those of the Ashton name.'

'Not really.'

A waiter approached before she could ask him to elaborate. Flynn ordered them wine, then asked for recommendations for food and ordered them without ever opening the menu, which Helena respected. For herself, she took the suggestion of *risotto alla Milanese* to start, but stuck with her *porcetta* for the main course.

As soon as the waiter had cleared the table, though, Helena pressed the point. 'What do you mean—not really?'

'Hmm?' Flynn had his phone out of his pocket again, but placed it face down on the table when she spoke.

'You said "not really" when I talked about you growing up with the expectations of the Ashton name. What did you mean?'

Flynn shrugged. 'Just the obvious. I'm not a real Ashton.'

'Of course you are! I mean, I know your father…' She trailed off. How exactly could she describe the way Ezekiel Ashton treated his sons? 'I know he wasn't always exactly even-handed with you and Zeke.'

'You mean he played us off against each other.' Flynn's voice was still even, but he stabbed at the nearest olive rather forcefully with the little stick. 'I know exactly why he gave me the job that was always promised to Zeke when I graduated. He wanted Zeke to have to fight me for it.'

'Except Zeke left instead.'

'And I stayed.' Another olive suffered a violent and pointy end.

'Why?' She'd wondered before, of course. Not originally, but ever since Zeke came back. She'd never got the full story, although she suspected Thea had. But either way, what had happened between Zeke and their father had influenced Flynn's life hugely. If she wanted to understand her husband, she had to understand that.

Flynn paused, a poor, defenceless olive halfway to his mouth. 'Where else would I go?'

'Anywhere, I suppose. Zeke did.'

'No. I…owed my father. Whatever else he did, and whatever his reasons, he took me in and gave me a home and a future when my real parents offered me neither.' A chill settled around Helena's heart at his words. 'I always knew that my place would be working at Morrison-Ashton, wherever I could be of most use.'

'You don't…' Helena swallowed, imagining a younger version of Flynn, always so neat and sensible and *kind*. Was it all because of a sense of debt? Had his adoption really coloured his whole life that way?

Had her daughter's?

And how would Flynn react when he found out about her past?

'You shouldn't have to sacrifice your own life and happiness to the company, though,' she managed in the end. 'Wasn't there ever anything else you wanted to do?'

Flynn shrugged. 'I never really considered it.'

'That's…that's awful.'

With a gentle smile, Flynn shook his head. 'Not really. Finding a place at the company…that was always the key for me, the way to assure my place in the family, too. But, in the end, that wasn't enough. Even Zeke turning the CEO role over to me… Our father had spent so long making it clear that it was meant for Zeke, that it had to stay in the family, it wouldn't have been enough.' He looked up and met her eyes, and Helena felt the warmth from them before he took her hand between his. '*You* made it possible for me to be a part of the family. Marrying you…you have given me the place I always wanted. And I need you to keep it.'

CHAPTER SEVEN

THOSE BLUEBELL EYES were so very wide Flynn wondered if he might have pushed too far. But it was important that Helena understood exactly how serious he was about making this marriage work, even if it meant partially explaining why.

He didn't want her pity, or to spill his bleeding heart story all over her. But if they were going to make a future as husband and wife, she had to know him. As he needed to know her, he supposed. And, after today, he hoped he was getting closer to that.

'Look. Zeke gave me the position that was always meant to be his, and our father had to accept that. I don't expect him to like it, ever, but it is now a fact. Before long there'll be contracts—'

'And we all know that paperwork is king,' Helena interjected, a wry smile on her lips.

'Indeed. The world has changed now, and so has the company. I want to be…worthy of that. I want to use this opportunity to bring Morrison-Ashton fully into the twenty-first century, build it up to even greater heights. I want to make our fathers proud. I want to make my wife proud.'

She glanced away at that, but her fingers tightened around his just for a moment. Almost, Flynn thought. He almost had her, and all he'd had to do was tell the truth.

'You've got it all planned out,' she murmured.

'I like to know where I'm going,' he said with a shrug. 'I find it helps make up for never knowing where I came from.'

Her eyes widened, and her gaze fixed on his face. 'Do you really feel that?'

'Sometimes.' Flynn frowned a little. 'Why?'

'I don't know. I just…' She took a breath, and he could almost see her trying to calm herself. But why? His adoption had never been a secret and, living as closely as their families had, none of this could really be considered a surprise. 'I always knew you were adopted, and I realised before I was very old that it made Ezekiel treat you differently. But you were always one of the family to me—to us. Even to Isabella, I think. And Zeke…'

'I've made my peace with Zeke,' Flynn said, remembering the last conversation he'd had with his brother before he left. Before he took Flynn's bride with him.

'Even now?'

'Especially now.' He stroked the back of her

hand lightly, just enough to remind her that they were connected now. 'Zeke didn't take Thea; she chose to go. And yes, that might not have been in my plan. But, as a result, I got to marry a beautiful, bright, wonderful woman. One who always considered me family, which means more than you can know. Trust me, I'm happy with how things turned out.'

'Oh!' It was more a surprised squeak than a word, and Flynn would have laughed at the shock on her face if it wouldn't have ruined the mood.

He released her hand and leant back as the waiter appeared with their starters. He had a feeling the conversation wasn't done yet, but he'd said what he needed to. She knew where he stood now. All he needed was for her to join him.

Easy.

He took a bite of his *crostini di fegato* while she toyed with her risotto, her fork twirling through the rice grains without ever making it near her mouth. She'd talk when she was ready, he decided, and set about enjoying his starter instead.

He was halfway through when she said, 'The other night…' then stopped and winced.

Of course. Their wedding night. Of course she'd want to talk about that in a crowded restaurant where he couldn't do anything to persuade her that his reluctance to take her to bed had nothing to do with lack of interest.

'It had been a long day for both of us,' he said as neutrally as he could.

She waved a hand at him across the table, dismissing his words as unnecessary or irrelevant, he wasn't completely sure which. 'That night, I thought for a moment that you might have been in love with my sister.'

Flynn blinked at her in confusion. 'Why on earth would you think that?'

The burst of laughter Helena didn't quite manage to contain by slapping her hand to her mouth drew the attention of every other diner in the room. Flynn steadfastly refused to look at or acknowledge them, keeping his gaze on Helena as she simmered down to a giggle.

'You realise how ridiculous that is, right? You were supposed to marry her four days ago, and you can't imagine how I might have got the impression that you were in love with her?'

Put like that, he supposed she had a point. 'Except you knew that the marriage was a business arrangement.'

'For her, yes. But I'd never spoken to you about how you felt. Still haven't, actually.' She paused in a way that suggested he was supposed to remedy that. Immediately. Except at that point the waiter returned to clear their starters, followed by another server carrying their main courses.

Flynn sighed and picked up his wine glass, taking the opportunity to consider his answer. Once they were alone again, he said, 'Marrying Thea was the plan because it gave us both what we wanted—or at least what I thought she wanted. Business and personal security, a future together and the possibility of children. Plus a good boost for the company PR. She got to escape her ridiculous failures with men, and I got to earn a real place at the family table. It worked.'

'So, nothing about love at all?' Helena pressed her fork into her *porcetta*, cut a sliver and popped it into her mouth. 'Mmm, this is delicious.'

'I'll admit I hoped that one day we might come to love one another. But no, I wasn't in love with her.' And it was painfully obvious to all and sundry that she hadn't been in love with him either. That was the only part that still smarted, just a little. Flynn turned his attention to his main course, mostly to pretend that it didn't.

'But you'd spoken about…children. And you admitted that you would have slept with her already, if she'd gone through with the marriage.' Her neutral tone gave nothing away, no hint of the right answer for him to give. Even if she hadn't really asked a question.

'For me, and for Thea, I think, we wanted to make this a real lasting marriage. Even if it didn't start out from a place of true love or anything. She's an attractive woman,' he added, watching

Helena's face closely as he spoke for any sign of a negative reaction. Sometimes when women said they wanted honesty, in his experience, they wanted anything but. 'And we had an iron-clad fidelity clause. If either of us ever wanted to have sex again, it had to be with each other.'

Helena sat back and studied him, sipping from her own wine glass. 'I like our story better,' she said after a moment.

'Our story?'

'Yes. It's more...dramatic. Romantic. Spontaneous.'

'Of course.' Flynn's shoulder muscles relaxed a little now she hadn't thrown wine in his face for talking about sleeping with her sister. 'And you like romance and spontaneity.'

'Who doesn't?' She gave a small shrug. 'But you two would have gone into that marriage with a heavy weight of expectations—written and signed in blood.'

'I like to think of it as more of a plan,' Flynn said mildly.

'You mean a schedule.' Helena shook her head. 'But life doesn't work like that. What if you slept together and it was dreadful?'

Flynn *really* didn't want to talk about this, but apparently he didn't have much of a choice. 'Then we'd have...I don't know. Practised, or something.' Could this be more awkward?

'What if she couldn't have children?' There was something behind Helena's eyes as she spoke, something he'd have missed if he hadn't been watching so closely. Was she trying to tell him something? He really hoped not.

'Then we'd figure something out. IVF or surrogacy. Adoption, maybe.' As a last resort. If he ever had to adopt, though, he'd do it differently. It would be about giving another lost child the sort of chances he'd had—but without the baggage. Not about what that child could give him.

'What if she fell in love with someone else?'

'Then she'd probably run away with him on our wedding morning.' A joke, but only just.

Helena rolled her eyes. 'I mean after the wedding.'

'Then we'd have…' The thought had never really occurred to him. The marriage was such an escape for both of them, to put them in a position where they didn't *have* to take the risk of love, that he couldn't imagine either of them looking for it outside of their union. 'We'd have talked about it. Sorted something out.'

'Like we're talking now,' Helena said. 'And since you're married to me, not her, I suppose we need to make some decisions about these things.'

And there it was. Everything he wanted, needed and he hadn't even had to ask for it. By the time Henry arrived with the new marriage contract, she'd be ready to sign, Flynn was sure of it.

'Just when I was celebrating our story for being different,' she said with a sigh.

He could afford to give her a little ground now, Flynn decided. He wanted her to be happy, after all. 'What did you like best about our story?'

'Oh, I don't know. The…immediacy of it, I guess. That we got married on a moment's notice, without all that paperwork and advance planning. If we were actually in love, it would be the most romantic thing ever. As it is…I guess it wasn't incredibly sensible.'

'Maybe not,' Flynn allowed. 'But I like to think it can work.'

'Yeah?' She'd finished eating, Flynn realised, and pushed her plate aside. The bottle of wine was almost empty too.

Maybe it was the wine that gave him the confidence to say, 'I want with you everything I ever wanted with Thea. Maybe even more. I want us to have a real marriage, and I hope that we will fall in love. But I need to know that you'll stick with it. That you'll give us a chance.'

Helena's bluebell eyes were wide and he could see the indecision in them, even if he couldn't fathom her reasons for holding back. She worried her lower lip with her teeth for a moment, and Flynn realised he was actually holding his breath. Waiting for his own wife to tell him she wanted to be married to him.

How had it come to this?

'I will,' Helena said eventually, so soft he almost didn't hear. Then she added, stronger this time, 'Yes, Flynn Ashton, I will stay married to you.'

This time, Flynn was pretty sure it was relief, rather than the wine, that caused his words. 'In that case, let's get out of here. I've got the perfect way to celebrate.'

A spur-of-the-moment idea, spontaneous and romantic—she was going to love it.

And suddenly that mattered an awful lot to him.

Flynn didn't let go of her hand all the way out to the car. Helena couldn't decide if the feel of his fingers wrapped around hers was comforting or terrifying.

What had she just done?

The whole idea was to stay married long enough to negate any scandal then get out, quick—preferably before Flynn discovered anything about her history that might ruin their friendship forever. Exes could be friends as long as they didn't screw up the marriage—or each other—too badly.

But now…now she was promising to stay with

him? To try and fall in love—as if that were even a thing people could do—and have a real life—a family!—with him. Everything she'd been avoiding for years.

As Flynn shut the car door after her, letting go of her hand long enough to whisper something to the driver before getting in the other side, Helena closed her eyes and let her head fall back.

Why? What had possessed her to do it?

Well, that one was probably easy enough. Guilt more than anything. Hearing Flynn talk so honestly about what he wanted from this marriage and why… How could she not want to give him that? To give him a place in their family. To give him the one thing he'd always needed most and never had—a place to belong.

Maybe it was partly a decade-old crush, partly that he'd always been a friend to her. But a large chunk of it, she knew, had to do with a tiny baby girl she'd never even been allowed to hold.

Flynn could never find out about the daughter she'd given away. He'd never understand. And if he wanted a family…well, he'd said himself that he'd consider surrogacy, or even adoption. He hadn't sounded thrilled at the idea, but still. Maybe she'd never even have to explain how the idea of another child growing inside her made her feel physically sick and her body start to shake.

Maybe he'd never need to know what she'd done.

Or maybe, just maybe, he'd understand. Not immediately, of course—she was under no illusion about that. But he wanted this marriage, wanted real love to grow between them.

Maybe all she needed to do was to build a relationship strong enough to withstand the truth, when it finally came out. Not an easy task, admittedly. But maybe not completely impossible.

'You okay over there?' Flynn asked, and when she opened her eyes he was leaning across the middle seat in the back of the car, looking at her.

She forced a smile. 'I'm fine. Where are we going?'

'It's a surprise.' Flynn sat back, looking smug. 'A spontaneous, unplanned, romantic surprise.'

'That your PA planned?' she guessed.

But Flynn shook his head. 'Nope. This one is all me. And I think you're going to love it.'

She probably would, Helena thought. It seemed that Flynn Ashton could convince her of whatever he set his mind to. And she couldn't deny the spark of pleasure that Flynn doing something off schedule, just for her, gave her.

She didn't realise where they were going until the car started over the bridge into the town nearest their villa. She'd been there before with Thea, had planned to come back and do some shopping herself. But she still couldn't imagine what Flynn planned for them to do there.

Maybe they were checking into a hotel. Maybe he'd decided to celebrate their new arrangement by consummating their marriage and didn't want to do it in the bed he was supposed to have shared with her sister.

Helena glanced over at Flynn. He didn't look like a man anticipating having sex within the hour. And, if she was honest, he didn't seem like the type to drag her off to a hotel without discussing it first.

One thing she'd learned in less than a week of marriage—her husband liked to talk things through. Who knew?

The car pulled into a row of parking spaces right by the central *piazza* and the driver opened her door. Helena stepped out, just as Flynn arrived to take her hand again.

'Now can you tell me?' she asked, but he shook his head.

'Soon,' he promised. Tugging on her hand, he led her across the *piazza*, towards a little side street, dodging cars speeding round corners and pedestrians too busy talking on their phones to look where they were going. The air smelled of strong coffee and sunshine, and it was almost enough for Helena to put all her worries aside.

The shade of the side street soothed her warm

skin and Helena's eyes widened in delight at the array of tiny shops, each selling everything from watches to leather goods to dresses and scarves. But Flynn obviously had a very clear idea of where he was going and allowed no time for window-shopping.

Even off-plan, Flynn Ashton didn't dawdle. Helena sighed. Maybe she could teach him.

'Here,' Flynn said and stopped so suddenly that Helena barely avoided crashing into him. As it was, she found herself staring into a shop window with her side pressed up against his, their joined hands tangled between them. She blamed his closeness for the long moments it took her to realise what she was looking at.

'A jewellery shop?' she asked, tearing her gaze away from the sparkly treasures in the window to look up at her husband.

'Yes. I thought…well, the romantic and spontaneous nature of our wedding meant that you never got an engagement ring. I thought we could choose one together, to celebrate.' He shuffled ever so slightly, from one foot to the other. Was he…no, really, was he nervous? Maybe that was why he avoided spontaneity—in case it went wrong.

An engagement ring. A little after the fact, but still. It would be something just for her—something that wasn't Thea's first.

She really liked that.

'I think that's a lovely idea,' Helena said, squeezing Flynn's fingers between her own. Then, impulsively, she stretched up on her toes to kiss him—not on the cheek like the sort of brother or friend he'd always been, but right on the lips. It was short but sweet, and enough to let him know that she was embracing her new role, she hoped. 'Let's go in.'

Inside, the cramped little shop felt too warm despite the dim lighting and shady spot. Laid out in glass counters sat tray after tray of diamond solitaire rings, varying slightly in design and shape and style, but all very clearly appropriate engagement rings.

'I spotted this shop walking through town the other day,' Flynn murmured as Helena took in the racks of sparkles. 'I just remembered it at lunch. Looks like it's just the place for what we're looking for.'

'It does,' Helena agreed, even as disappointment tugged at her belly. How was she supposed to pick one ring to symbolise their whole future life together when they were all basically the same? Which tiny variation might make the difference to her happy ever after?

A neatly dressed woman stepped out from a back office behind the counter and smiled as she offered to let Helena try some on. Flynn smiled his encouragement as the shop assistant unlocked the cases and took out the first tray.

Helena blinked as more diamonds than she'd ever imagined caught the light and sparkled up at her.

Well, maybe she'd just have to try some on. Surely she'd know the right one when she found it?

Somewhere around tray three, or ring thirty-six, Helena began to doubt her theory. Flynn had wandered off to the other side of the shop, leaving Helena and the increasingly bored assistant to wade through all the diamonds alone.

'They're all beautiful,' Helena said apologetically, for what must have been the sixth time. 'I just…I'm looking for one that feels right. You know?'

'Of course,' the assistant said in her thick Italian accent. 'You will wear this ring forever. It must be perfect.'

'Exactly,' Helena said, her fingers clenching at the word 'forever'. She sighed. 'Why don't we try this one again?' It *was* beautiful. Simple, elegant… Helena couldn't figure out what was wrong with it.

Flynn appeared over her shoulder, frowning. 'Not that one,' he said. 'Looks too much like—'

'Thea's,' Helena finished, the problem suddenly clear. Slipping the ring off again, she placed it back in the tray and moved over to the next one.

'Hang on,' Flynn said. Helena glanced up—he was across the other side of the tiny shop again and this time he had the assistant with him, unlocking another cabinet. 'I want to try something.'

Helena frowned, but waited as instructed. Grinning, Flynn crossed the room with his fist clenched tightly around something. 'Close your eyes.'

'Really?'

'Yep.'

He looked so pleased with himself that she couldn't help but do as he asked. She felt him take her left hand and slip a ring on to the fourth finger.

'And it even fits perfectly,' Flynn said. 'Okay, open your eyes.'

Helena stared at the jewel on her finger. 'That's not a diamond.'

'Well, no. I mean, obviously, if that's what you want, there's plenty to choose from here. I just thought...'

'No, no. I mean—it's not a diamond! I couldn't figure out why the other rings weren't right, but now I get it. I wasn't looking for a diamond.' Helena grinned. It all seemed so obvious now that Flynn had solved it for her.

The shop assistant muttered something in Italian that Helena couldn't understand but guessed probably meant: *Why couldn't she have figured that out half an hour ago?*

Relief flooded Flynn's features. 'Oh, good. I just…that one made me think of you. I don't know—maybe it's because it's blue.'

'Sapphire,' Helena said.

'Whatever. It reminded me of your eyes. And I know it's not traditional, but neither is buying the engagement ring after the wedding.'

'It's perfect.' Helena tilted her finger to make it sparkle in the dim overhead lights. 'I love it.'

'Great. Then hand it over.' He held out his hand, palm up.

'What?' Helena curled her fingers in to keep her ring right where it was, thank you very much.

'You can't wear it yet,' Flynn said with exaggerated patience. 'I need to propose properly with it.'

'You also need to pay for it.' The shop assistant gave them a not entirely patient smile, and Flynn laughed.

'Very true. Perhaps we can have a ring box?'

As the shop assistant rang up the total, Helena reluctantly slipped her sapphire off her finger and placed it in the velvet box on the counter. Everything about this marriage might be backwards, she thought, but that didn't mean it couldn't work.

Flynn had picked out her perfect ring when

she didn't even know what she was looking for. What other marvels might he work in her life if she gave him the chance?

They were almost home when his phone rang.

'I'm sorry,' Flynn said, yanking it out of his pocket. 'Do you mind?'

Helena shook her head. 'Go on. I think you've earned at least one business call today.'

He flashed her a smile as he answered. He knew that the engagement ring idea was a good one. When in doubt, buy jewellery—his mother's entire contribution to his education about how to treat women might not have been lengthy, but it worked.

'Henry. I hope you're calling with good news.' And flight numbers, preferably. He wanted everything he and Helena had discussed down on paper before anything changed. And especially before they had to go back to London and deal with their families again. If anything was going to screw things up between them, Flynn would place money on it being Ezekiel Ashton—even if he didn't mean to.

'Afraid not.' Henry sounded harassed. Henry never sounded anything other than cool and collected, even when Flynn woke him up at two in the morning. This was not a good sign. 'Can you talk?'

The car swept up the driveway of the villa, stopping right by the front door. 'Yeah, I can talk. Just one moment.'

'Let me guess,' Helena said as the driver cut the engine. 'You need to work.'

'Just a little. But we'll have dinner together?'

'Definitely.' Helena grinned. 'You've got something to give me later.'

'That's right, I do.' Once again, jewellery saved him from himself. 'I'll see you for dinner.' Opening the car door, he stepped out and strode towards the villa. 'Henry? I'm here. What's happening?'

'I need you to make a decision about priorities,' Henry said as Flynn let himself into the villa and headed for the room his father had been using as his study. Ezekiel wasn't there any more and it only made sense for him to use it. The symbolism of taking over his father's desk was purely accidental, if rather satisfying.

'Priorities?' Flynn sat himself in the desk chair. With his laptop and files set up down there it already felt more like his own space. He'd already spent a decent amount of time there and, with another week or so of their honeymoon to go, the chances were he'd be spending a lot more. Just not so much as to alienate Helena.

See? He had his priorities straight.

'Which is more important to you: your post-nuptial agreement or the contracts for the sale of This Minute to Morrison-Ashton?' Henry asked.

'You mean the contracts that compel my father to make me CEO, in return for Zeke selling us his company,' Flynn clarified. They both knew his interest in those contracts of sale had less to do with the digital media company his brother had built up and more to do with his own future at Morrison-Ashton. 'Why? What's gone wrong with them?'

'Your father is contesting rather a lot of the details.' Flynn got the impression that Henry was understating things there. Ezekiel Ashton would fight tooth and nail to retain control of that company until they put him in his grave. But Flynn had faith in Zeke. He'd said it was a done deal and that meant it would be, eventually—however hard and long their father fought it. 'Your brother's legal team are doing an admirable job, but I think you might want me here to help smooth the path from our side. Just to make sure that he doesn't manage to slip anything in there that could hold up his stepping down from the CEO position.'

'Henry, are you trying to get out of a paid holiday in Tuscany for a couple of days?' Flynn kicked his feet up on the desk and leant back in his desk chair.

Henry laughed. 'I might be trying to not gatecrash your honeymoon, but only for business reasons, I promise you.'

'Well, I'm afraid you're going to have to gatecrash,' Flynn told him. 'We've got to get that marriage contract signed.'

'Things going that badly, huh?' Henry asked, his tone sympathetic.

'The opposite, actually.' Flynn let himself remember the look on Helena's face when she'd seen her ring. 'It's going very, very well. And I don't want to give my father the chance to ruin that.'

'You think he will?' Henry sounded surprised. 'I know he wasn't entirely happy about you marrying the wrong sister, but does it really make that much difference?'

'Do you know, Henry, I think it will. To me, anyway.' He couldn't say how. It had been less than a week. But already his relationship with Helena felt more like a…well…relationship than things with Thea ever had.

'You're sounding smitten, my friend.'

'I'm a newlywed,' Flynn joked. 'I'm supposed to be besotted with my wife. Whoever she turns out to be.'

Henry laughed. 'Well, okay, then. But if things are so hunky-dory with the new Mrs Ashton, what's the worry?'

'It was made very clear to me by my father and

his esteemed business partner that unless I return from this trip with a signed and notarised post-nuptial agreement, they would take it into their own hands to get one. I want this marriage to be on my terms—mine and Helena's. That means we need you here to make that legal.'

'Fair enough.' Flynn heard the clicking of a mouse on the other end of the line. 'Best flight I can get has me with you tomorrow mid-morning. Will that work?'

'Perfect.' That gave him tonight to wine and dine Helena, propose, kiss her goodnight. Just one more frustrated night in his own bed and then they could sign the papers and make this a real marriage at last.

'I'll get it booked,' Henry promised. 'But, Flynn…make sure you're both on the same page before I get there, yeah? You know these things always go more smoothly when there are no surprises.'

'I know. Don't worry. Helena and I aren't the secretive types.' Compared to Thea, Helena was an open book. And he didn't have any more brothers for her to declare undying love for, so he figured he was probably safe there too.

'Then I'll see you two lovebirds tomorrow,' Henry said and hung up.

Flynn dropped his phone on to the desk and pulled the ring box out of his pocket, opening it to admire the deep blue stone at the heart of the ring. He'd clear his emails and then still have time to shower and change before dinner.

He smiled to himself. Just another hour or so and it would be time to propose to his wife.

CHAPTER EIGHT

HELENA WOUND THE last string of lights along the beams of the terrace and stood back to admire her handiwork. Not bad, if she did say so herself. The table for two—complete with white linen napkins and flickering candlelight—was all prepared, and the fairy lights she'd found left over from the wedding decorations were perfect for giving their little terrace dinner table the right romantic atmosphere—far better than they'd managed in the formal dining room the last few days. The flowers climbing the stone walls added a heady, spicy scent in the last of the day's sunlight, and the air was still warm enough that she didn't need the wrap she'd brought out with her.

She smoothed down her blue silk dress and tucked a blonde curl behind her ear. She was ready, the table was ready. The wine she'd brought from Gia's vineyard was open on the table, ready for pouring, and the cook had promised her that dinner would be ready at exactly seven-thirty.

It was the perfect night to get engaged.

All she needed now was her husband.

She turned to let the warm evening breeze brush over her skin as she stared out across the beautiful Tuscan countryside. It was almost a shame to have to go back to London at all, she thought. Out here, all things seemed possible.

Possible enough that she'd put on her best lingerie under her dress, anyway.

'Okay, this kind of spontaneous romance I am absolutely in favour of.'

Helena turned at the sound of Flynn's voice and found him leaning against the doorway between the terrace and the house, his gaze fixed not on the romantic trappings she'd set up, but firmly upon her.

'Actually,' she admitted, 'this is the kind of romance that takes planning. I got Gia to smuggle the wine into the car when you were preoccupied with your phone earlier.'

'So, you were planning this even before our ring-shopping expedition?' Flynn stepped closer and Helena could feel her skin warming and the little fine hairs on her arms standing up as he grew nearer. How had she never known how he affected her until she married him?

'Long before. Can't a girl want a romantic night in with her husband?'

'She most certainly can.' He put a hand on her waist and Helena only just resisted the urge to snuggle up close against his chest. 'Especially when she wears a dress like yours.'

'You like it?' She stepped back far enough to give him a quick twirl, the silky pleats of her dress rising up a little around her thighs as she turned.

'I adore it. You look beautiful. Even more beautiful than you did in the vineyard earlier, with the sun in your hair and your gorgeous bright smile.'

'You thought I was beautiful then?' That had also been before their conversation in the restaurant—before she'd agreed to stay with him. Maybe he had more reasons to want her to stay than just his plans for the future.

Maybe he did really want *her* to stay, not just any girl bearing the right surname.

'I couldn't believe I'd never seen quite how beautiful you are before.' His gaze locked with hers as he spoke, and his irises seemed lit up by the fading sunlight until they looked like poured caramel. Helena swayed closer to him without thinking, as if there was simply nowhere else she should or could be. He caught her around the waist, arms strong and warm as he pulled her near.

'You know, I had a big lunch...' Helena trailed off as she licked her lips, and watched Flynn's Adam's apple bob as he swallowed.

He wanted her. He wanted her as much as she

wanted him and, whatever his reasons for sending her to bed like a child on their wedding night, tonight, this night, he was hers. One way or another she was taking her husband to bed—before she lost her nerve completely.

Or so she thought until he dropped his arms from her waist and stepped away.

'Dinner is served!' The maid stepped on to the terrace, plates in her hands, and Flynn strode across to pull Helena's chair out for her.

Helena pouted at him, and he laughed. The maid, forehead creased, wisely placed their meals on the table and disappeared back into the villa.

'Come on, sit down.' Flynn rattled her chair a little against the stone of the terrace. 'I want to do this properly.'

'I suppose.' Helena took her seat, let Flynn push her chair in. At least she'd asked the cook for just a pasta main and a pudding, since they'd had lunch out already. Maybe they could take the dessert up to bed with them...

The long strands of pasta, wrapped in a deeply savoury *ragu*, were delicious, Helena had to admit. As she twirled them expertly around her fork and sipped at the gorgeous red wine, courtesy of Gia, she thought there were worse ways to spend the evening.

'So, is London missing you, then?' she asked,

thinking of the phone call that had dragged him from her earlier.

'Oh, I expect they're enjoying the peace, quite honestly.' Flynn gave her a half smile. 'Apart from my solicitor, who I woke up at two o'clock the other morning.'

'So *that's* who you were calling. I did wonder who could be important enough to let me go up to bed alone...' Helena watched his face closely as she spoke and yes, there it was. A hint of uncertainty, an uncomfortable twist of the mouth.

She put down her fork.

He'd asked her to spend her life with him. They'd bought a ring. He'd called her beautiful... and he still didn't plan to sleep with her tonight.

There was definitely something odd going on here.

'That's who was calling earlier, too,' Flynn went on, as if Helena hadn't just uncovered a problem of major proportions in their marriage. 'Apparently my father is being difficult about the contracts for the sale of This Minute, as expected. Nothing to worry about, though. Zeke's legal team are, by all accounts, very capable.'

'That's good.' Somehow, she had a feeling that the people Zeke would have put on the job wouldn't just be capable. They'd be relentless, and they'd take Ezekiel Ashton for everything they wanted before they gave him what Zeke had promised.

She didn't have a problem with that, actually. Especially after her conversation with Flynn at lunchtime.

No, Helena's only problem so far this evening was a husband who didn't want to sleep with her—or wouldn't let himself want it. And that was far more important right now than a manipulative father-in-law with a Zeus complex.

They finished their pasta in companionable silence, but Helena barely tasted it. Any moment now, she knew, Flynn was going to get down on one knee and present her with the most perfect ring and ask her to share her life with him.

But how could she promise to do that without finding out if they were compatible in bed? If she could relax enough to let herself be with him? Or if there was some reason she should know about that meant they might never even find out?

The maid cleared their dishes silently. Flynn smiled at her and said, 'We'll wait a moment on dessert, if that's okay. I'll call you when we're ready,' and Helena knew this was it.

She'd dreamt, as a younger girl, about proposals—maybe even more than she'd dreamt about weddings and wedding nights. She'd imagined herself falling in love, having some handsome man drop to his knees and beg her to marry him.

She'd even thought about the perfect way to respond—amazed joy, she'd decided, was best. Hand to the mouth, perhaps, and an enthusiastic, *Of course I will!*

She'd never imagined it would be like this.

'I know this isn't going to come as much of a surprise to you.' Flynn reached into his pocket and pulled out the ring box, grinning at her all the while. 'But I want you to have the full experience. So…' He stood up, moved around to her side of the table and gracefully lowered himself to one knee. 'Helena Juliette Ashton. Would you do me the incredible honour of agreeing to remain my wife and live our very own happily ever after together?'

Amazed joy, Helena tried to remind herself. Enthusiasm. Happiness. Saying yes.

But instead, what came out of her mouth was, 'Why don't you want to sleep with me?'

'What on earth could have given you that idea?' Flynn asked, his hand still holding out the open ring box. Helena merely raised her eyebrows at him and watched as his gaze slid from her face down to that perfect sapphire. 'Trust me—I want to make love to you very much.'

Helen frowned. He was telling the truth. Hadn't she seen it in his eyes, felt it in his touch, known it even when he'd kissed her after the speeches on their wedding day? So maybe she was asking the wrong question.

'Okay then, why won't you?'

'Is this really the time you want to have this conversation?'

'I think it's something that shouldn't wait any longer,' Helena said. 'But you can, you know, stand up if that's easier.'

'Right. Because that's the biggest problem with this conversation.' Nevertheless, Flynn pushed himself up to standing then dragged his chair across to sit beside her.

'So?' she asked when he sat looking at her, not saying anything.

Flynn sighed. 'So. Of course I want to sleep with you. You're my wife. You're beautiful. I care about you and I hope to have a future with you. But…'

Oh, no. Where was this going? Even in her panic, Helena didn't believe for a second that he hadn't done it before, and she knew he wasn't in love with Thea, so what was it? Even if he had some purity, 'waiting until marriage' thing going on, they were already married!

'Before we take that step, before we start something that will hopefully lead to a deeper affection between us, I think it's important that we agree certain things about our future together.'

Helena blinked. 'Isn't that what we did at

lunch? What we're doing now, with the ring and all?'

'Partly,' Flynn said. Why wasn't he meeting her eyes? 'But, for it to be truly official, we do need the post-nuptial agreement to be signed and filed. Should anything happen, it's important that these things have been formalised.'

Helena stared at him. 'Flynn. Please, please tell me that you're not refusing to sleep with me because of *paperwork*.'

Dropping his head to stare at his hands, Flynn gave a sort of half laugh. 'It does sound that way, doesn't it?'

'Wanna try and make it sound a different way?' Helena suggested.

'Okay.' Flynn sucked in a deep breath and sat back in his chair, letting the air out slowly. A delaying tactic, Helena recognised. He was figuring out the best way to say whatever he had to say, which meant she probably wasn't going to like it.

'The other night, before you came in wearing that incredible satin thing—that's still upstairs, right? I really want to see you in that again some time when I can appreciate it properly.'

'It is.' A faint warmth hit Helena's cheeks. So far he wasn't doing so badly.

'Good. Anyway. Before that, I had a meeting with our fathers that left me in a...not great mood. But it also got me thinking.' He looked up, his serious eyes focused on hers. 'The moment we sleep together, we've changed the game. There's no hope of an annulment when we get back. You have to be sure that it's what you want.'

'An annulment?' Helena shook her head a little to try and make sense of it. 'You were refusing to sleep with me to make sure I had an out?'

'That was one reason.'

'What was the other?'

'My father suggested that, should I have any problems getting you to agree to the same terms as Thea for the marriage, I should just get you pregnant to tie you to me, then make sure you signed before the child was born.'

Helena's heart froze in her chest. 'What did my father say?' she asked. Because Ezekiel probably never knew what she'd been through, and she expected that kind of callousness from him anyway. But her own father...

'He... Helena, he laughed. He said something about you making up for the past by marrying me, and he laughed when Dad told me to get you pregnant.' He ran a shaking hand through his hair, and Helena wanted to hold him, to soothe him. To have him soothe her. But all she could hear in her mind was her father's laughter, dismissing the most important thing—the worst thing—that had ever happened to her as a joke.

She'd known that she and Thea were often

more useful than loved. She'd understood that this marriage was a business deal, convenient and lucrative rather than something to be celebrated.

But until this moment she'd never realised quite how little her father thought of her. And suddenly her heart felt as if it had been torn apart.

'I couldn't bear it.' Flynn was still talking, and Helena tried to pay him proper attention again. 'They were just so casual about the idea—about a child's life. And I knew I couldn't risk that. That we had to be sure, that everything had to be agreed before anything like that could happen.'

Helena swallowed and it felt as if there was a rock stuck in her throat. He hadn't wanted her to be trapped, hadn't wanted any child to be unwanted, or used, like he had been. Her soul ached for the boy Flynn must have been, and for the man he'd become. Her own battered heart reached out for his. Maybe they really could give each other what they'd lacked so far, all their lives—love.

He wanted so badly to do this right, to make a perfect future for them. And so what if he planned it out moment by moment? His reasons were good. His heart was good.

And Helena wanted that heart for her own. More than she'd ever done as a fourteen-year-old child. More even than when she'd envied her sister her golden, good fiancé. More than when she'd stepped into that borrowed wedding dress, and more certainly than when she'd propositioned him in her negligee on their wedding night. More still than when he'd chosen her the perfect engagement ring.

She was in love with her own husband, and it scared her and filled her more than she'd ever known anything could.

'I think you should ask me that question again now,' she said, nerves making her whole body feel as if it was vibrating from the inside out. She needed to tell him the truth, needed to confess. But if she did…it could destroy the cautious happiness they were building together. Once they were home, once the paperwork was signed, maybe then she could talk about what had happened to her, what she'd done. Maybe then she could make him understand.

But first she had to make him love her.

Flynn smiled up at her, already on his knees again. 'Helena. Will you be my wife? In every way there is?'

'Yes,' she breathed and felt that amazed joy flooding through her.

Flynn swept her up in his arms the moment she spoke. He owed her a proper kiss, after their first public one, and that was what he intended to give her. Lowering his mouth to hers, he tried to convey everything he felt—every hope, every dream—through a kiss.

From her eager response, he hoped he had got pretty close.

It amazed him to think that just last week he hadn't known this woman—not really. He knew Helena, Thea's sister, or Helena, Thomas's daughter. But he had no idea of the wonder, the humour, the warmth and the beauty that lay beyond those labels.

'I can't believe I came so close to marrying the wrong woman,' he murmured against her lips, and felt rather than saw her smile in response. 'This is it. This is exactly how it was meant to be all along.'

'I know,' Helena said, and he could hear her happiness in the words. 'I know. And we so almost didn't…'

'But we did. We have each other now.' It might not be love yet, Flynn thought, but he could see the pathway there. Could see every step between here and their future.

Helena pulled back a little, still smiling, her eyes glistening with unshed tears. 'You haven't even put the ring on me yet.'

'I haven't?' Flynn blinked, and saw it sitting on the table beside them. Pulling it free of its velvet box, he lifted Helena's left hand and slipped it on next to her wedding ring. 'There.'

'There,' Helena echoed, staring down at her hand. 'It really is the most beautiful ring I've ever seen.'

'For the most beautiful woman,' Flynn said, knowing it was corny and not even caring. Somehow this moment, alone on the terrace, felt more permanent, more official than the big church ceremony and the signed register. This was the moment he'd remember as their true wedding. The moment they understood each other and committed to their future.

Helena smiled up at him, then caught her lip between her teeth, the way he already knew she always did when she was deciding whether or not to say something.

'Go on,' he said. 'You may as well say whatever it is. After your response to my initial proposal, it's unlikely you can come up with anything worse.'

'True. And I do think you'll like this one more.' Swaying closer, she wrapped herself tighter around his body, pressing herself against him until it felt as if even air couldn't squeeze between them. His body began to react immediately, even before Helena rose up on her tiptoes, brushing against him every slow inch of the way, and whispered in his ear, 'So, do you want tiramisu for dessert? Or me?'

He swallowed, trying to cling on to the composure he was so famed for in the boardroom. The plan was to wait. He'd already pushed so far up against every line he'd drawn for himself. And there was more than business on the line here, he admitted to himself, more than money. He had to be sure he could risk his heart. 'Are you sure? The contract—'

'Paperwork's a formality,' she murmured against the skin of his neck, placing kisses between each word. 'I'm yours now, whatever happens. So take me.'

The words ripped through the last of his self-control and Flynn hauled her up his body into another kiss, this one harder, more desperate, more wanting.

'Upstairs,' he managed, just, as her hands clutched at his back. 'Now.'

He didn't need to say it twice.

It was several hours later, with the sky dark outside the bedroom window, that Flynn tugged her closer against his naked body and said, 'We never did get that tiramisu.'

Helena laughed against his skin, her hands still roaming over his chest. 'You never got me in that negligee, either.'

'Maybe tomorrow night,' Flynn said, yawning.

'Maybe,' Helena agreed, although she knew they'd never make it that far. By tomorrow night they'd be too desperate for each other again, too consumed with want that they'd forget all about her fancy nightie. Just as they had done tonight.

It had been more than she'd dreamt it could be. The way he moved against her, within her… the way he touched her, with a sort of reverence she'd never imagined a man could have for her body. As if he were drinking in every detail of her, and each one intoxicated him.

She should never have worried about them being compatible, and she almost laughed when she thought that, until a couple of hours ago, she'd honestly been afraid he hadn't wanted her.

She'd been scared, she admitted to herself, lying in the darkness in her husband's arms. She'd not wanted to think about it, but there had been very few men since she'd fallen pregnant at sixteen, and none that made Helena feel the way that Flynn did. She'd worried whether she'd be enough for him, worried more about protection until he'd pulled a condom from his wallet, and worried most that he'd be able to tell her secrets with one glance at her body.

He hadn't, though. And since his eyes and hands and mouth had covered every inch of her, she didn't imagine he would now.

Her past was locked away until she chose to share it with him. He'd be hurt, she knew, that she'd kept it from him, but she liked to think he'd understand. Especially now—they were already so close, and after so little time. By the time it mattered, when they talked again about children, they'd be a proper unit. A family, even. He'd understand.

And he'd understand, she thought, if she told him she wanted to adopt. He might even welcome it. As long as she got the timing right, they would make it work, she was sure of it.

They had to. She'd committed now, and so had he. There wasn't any room to step back any more.

'What are you thinking about?' Flynn asked, his voice sleepy as he kissed the top of her head. 'You're keeping me awake with all those thoughts.'

'I'm just thinking how happy I am,' Helena replied, and hoped he didn't know her well enough yet to tell when she was lying.

He didn't. 'Good,' he said, turning on to his side and pulling her back against his chest. Soon, his breathing evened out and she knew he was asleep.

But Helena lay awake almost until the sun crept over the window ledge, thinking about the things she'd done and the choices she'd made.

When Flynn awoke the next morning he knew instinctively that it wasn't six a.m. The sun sat too high in the sky, sending beams of warmth and light that cut across the bed. They hadn't shut the curtains the night before, he realised, and still he'd slept in well past his normal waking hour.

It had to be the exercise, he thought, stretching out aching muscles as far as he could without waking the woman sleeping in his arms.

His wife.

She'd been everything he'd dreamt she could be, and more. If he'd needed any extra proof that things had worked out for the best, he had it. As the mid-morning sun glinted off the sapphire on her finger, he knew that Helena was the one for him, for life. Whatever happened next—with his father, the company, even with Zeke and Thea—it would be him and Helena against the world. They had their own family. His hand slipped down to rest against her stomach for a moment. And one day, not yet, but once things were settled with the CEO role, that family would grow a little bigger.

He couldn't wait.

Flynn toyed with the idea of waking Helena to remind her again just how good they were together, but then his eye caught on a piece of card tucked in the edge of the mirror on her dressing table, just under the window. Squinting, he made out the words printed on the front and smiled when he realised what it was.

His wedding invitation. His and Thea's, defaced by Helena to turn it into theirs. And on the back, he knew, would be that impromptu contract she'd scrawled across it.

The contract. Henry was arriving today. Would be arriving—Flynn glanced at the clock next to the mirror—any moment now.

Reluctantly, he disentangled himself from Helena's pale limbs, smiling when she reached for him without waking. Tucking the blanket around her, he pulled on yesterday's jeans and headed for the room next door, where the shower wouldn't disturb her. He'd get dressed, hunt out some breakfast and meet with Henry. If they were quick, he could have the whole contract ready for signatures before Helena even woke up.

By the time he made it downstairs, Henry had not only arrived but had also befriended the maid and the cook. Flynn found him settled into one of the armchairs in the large hall area, a cup of coffee and a plate of pastries at his elbow. He folded the paper he was reading as he saw Flynn descending the stairs and tucked it away in his briefcase.

'Am I to assume that the urgency with which you required me to dance attendance on you has now passed?' Henry asked, a mocking smile on his face.

Flynn couldn't help but smile back. Henry had known him a long time, had worked with him almost since he'd started at Morrison-Ashton, and knew Flynn better than most. If anyone was going to be happy for him, it was probably Henry.

It was another sign of how little input he'd had on the wedding planning and guest list that Henry hadn't been invited. Maybe they should throw some sort of spectacular first anniversary party next year and invite all the people they'd have actually liked to be there. Poor Helena hadn't been allowed to invite *anyone* to her own wedding.

He should really make that up to her.

Flynn dropped into the chair opposite his friend and helped himself to one of the pastries. 'We still need the contract,' he said. 'But you're going to have to wait for my wife to wake up first. She's not good at mornings.' He tried to keep his expression blank as Henry studied him, but apparently failed as Henry shook his head and laughed.

'Oh, you lucky, lucky—' He broke off before the curse. 'Only you could get dumped on your wedding day and still end up with a beautiful bride you're madly in love with.'

'I didn't say love,' Flynn argued, but he couldn't help the grin that came at the thought, 'yet.'

'A couple of years' time, you're going to be running the company, making millions and have chubby toddlers chasing around after you. It's going to be sickening.'

'Perhaps,' Flynn agreed. 'Doesn't sound too bad to me.'

'It wouldn't. You're not the one who'll have to deal with you being so insufferably smug about it.' Henry flashed him a grin. 'Seriously, though, I'm happy for you. Nobody deserves this more than you.'

Was that true? Flynn suspected not. But the fact his friend thought so...that meant something. Maybe, after every bad start, everything he'd had to fight to get here, maybe this was his time to be happy at last.

He hoped so.

'Come on.' Flynn got to his feet. No point lingering on the sentimental when there was paperwork to deal with. 'Let's go through to the study and get started. I'll have the maid bring us some more coffee. I'd like to get this agreement put to bed before Helena wakes up, so she can sign it and forget it.'

'You mean so you can take her back to bed again,' Henry said.

'That too.'

'You know I have to go through all the details with her too, right? You can't just tell her to sign here and have done with it—however desperate you are to get her naked.'

Pretty desperate, Flynn had to admit. But not enough to ignore the law. 'I know. But I want to try and keep this one simple, if I can. Helena's not a huge fan of paperwork.'

Maybe, once Henry had gone, he'd take her over his father's desk in the study. Maybe that would endear her to paperwork a little bit more.

'And she married you?' Henry asked in mock astonishment. 'Heaven help her.'

Flynn ignored him. It was going to be another glorious day.

CHAPTER NINE

HELENA WOKE UP ALONE, stretching out in the bed like a starfish to work out the kinks and aches that her muscles had built up over the night. She wasn't used to sharing her space while she slept, although she was happy to learn if it meant sharing the bed with Flynn.

Where was Flynn, anyway?

Checking the clock, she saw it was already late morning, which meant he'd probably sloped off to work. Maybe she'd surprise him in his study, persuade him to come back to bed for a while. They could rerun the events of their wedding night, only with the right outcome this time...

She showered quickly, fixed her hair and cleaned her teeth, then dressed in the satin negligee Flynn had so wanted to see again. Then, just in case she ran into any or all of the household staff on her way down, she slipped on a light matching robe which made the whole ensemble *almost* decent.

Yawning, she opened the door and headed for the stairs, wondering if maybe she should stop for coffee first. No, husband first, then coffee. She could send him out to bring some back to the room afterwards. Ooh, breakfast in bed! That was what honeymoons were for. Well, amongst other things…

When she reached the study, she didn't bother to knock and didn't even register the two voices inside until she'd already opened the door.

'Oh! Sorry.' She pulled an apologetic face at Flynn, who smiled reassuringly. The man sitting across the desk from him, a laptop between them angled so they could both see the screen, laughed. It was a nice laugh, though, Helena thought. Not cruel or mocking, just amused.

'Don't worry,' he said, getting to his feet. 'We were actually waiting for you. I'm Henry, Flynn's solicitor.' He held out a hand for Helena to shake.

She frowned as she took it. 'Solicitor? Is there something wrong?' Then she realised, and groaned. 'Seriously, Flynn? Paperwork, at this time in the morning?'

'It's practically lunchtime,' Flynn pointed out.

'In his defence, I think he mostly wanted to get it sorted so that you could both get back to enjoying your honeymoon,' Henry said.

Rolling her eyes, Helena dropped into the third chair set around the desk. 'Fine. But I'm going to need coffee.'

It turned out that most of the post-nuptial

agreement—which sounded like a stupid name to Helena, but was apparently what the thing was called—was pretty boring. Flynn and Henry had already been through the document and updated the original to reflect the slight change in wedding plans. Helena found some comfort in knowing that these were things that Thea had agreed to, even agreed with. It made nodding along as Henry talked her through it much easier.

Their finances, the business; that was all straightforward in the end—the lengthy negotiations between Thea, Flynn and their fathers had already hammered all that out. So the contract mostly came down to the relationship between her and Flynn.

That part, at least, she understood.

'So, you're both still happy to live in the London townhouse we arranged, right?' Henry asked, and Helena nodded. 'Great. Next up, charitable and social obligations.'

Helena sighed. She really should have just stayed in bed. Flynn would have come and found her eventually.

When they reached the part about sexual relations, Flynn stared at the ceiling and Helena couldn't help but laugh.

'I'm guessing we can strike the part about negotiating the initiation of sexual relations in one year's time?' Henry asked, clearly unable to hide the amusement in his voice.

'Yeah, I think that ship has pretty much sailed,' Helena said with a grin.

'It was a stupid clause anyway,' Flynn added, his gaze still focused on the ceiling.

'Okay, then. In that case, the next bit is the declarations,' Henry said, scrolling down to the next page.

'Like the sickness and health part of the wedding?' Helena asked.

'Not exactly. Basically, we just need you to sign this section to say that you've never been married before, are not in a partnership with anyone else at this time, that you don't have any children by a previous relationship—things that would affect your finances or inheritances mostly.'

Helena's whole body trembled as if she had no control over it. She couldn't speak—every word she thought of stuck in her throat. Her skin burned as if she'd stepped too close to the fire—and maybe she had, in a way.

She'd known last night that she had to tell Flynn about her daughter, but not like this. Not now and not here, not with Henry listening in.

Not when everything was finally going so well.

'Helena? What's wrong?' Flynn was at her side now—when had he even moved? He took her hand, squeezing it gently, and Helena wanted nothing more than to cling on to it and never, ever let go. She'd come so close to getting everything she'd ever wanted.

And now one mistake from eight years ago was going to wreck it all.

In her mind, the film of the night she'd told Thea ran over and over. Her sister's tears, followed by her father's shouts. The ugly accusations, the hatred. And then the pity in Isabella's expression when she'd arrived, as she always did, to support Thomas above all else. Not just pity, though. A sense of inevitability, as if they'd all known Helena would screw up irrevocably in the end; it had only been a matter of time.

Thea was the only one who'd listened, who'd understood what had really happened that night. And their father had just blamed her for letting Helena out that night at all. As if Thea were more to blame than Helena, and Helena more to blame than the boys who—she stopped that thought. She couldn't relive that. Not now.

Instead, she remembered the coldness in her father's eyes as he'd told her they would fix this. That she would do exactly as she was told. He and Isabella had a plan and she would follow it to the letter. And, if she did, she could come home and live her normal life again. Afterwards.

As if she could ever be the same, after.

'Do you want me to call for someone?' Henry

asked, sounding concerned. 'Get some water or something?'

'Yeah, there should be someone in the kitchen.' Flynn placed the back of his hand against her forehead. 'Helena, talk to me. What is it? Are you feeling faint? I should have got you a proper breakfast. Let me ask Henry to—'

'No.' She couldn't take it any more. She couldn't let him carry on being so kind to her, not when he didn't know the truth. 'I don't need anything. But I can't…' She stumbled over the words as she tried to get to her feet. Her legs felt too weak to support her body, but she forced them to move, to take her away from here. 'I can't sign this.'

And then she ran, the image of Flynn's horrified face imprinted on her memory.

Okay, this…? This was *not* the plan.

Flynn stared after his wife as Helena stumbled out of the study and raced up the stairs. From the doorway, he could just about see the way she clung to the banister as she climbed, that stupid satin nightgown flapping around her legs.

'What happened?' Henry asked, striding across the hallway with a glass of water in his hand.

'I have no idea,' Flynn replied, gaze still locked on the now empty staircase. 'But I'm going to find out. Stay here.'

They had an agreement, he fumed silently as he took the stairs two at a time. They'd talked about everything, he'd opened up to her in ways he'd never imagined he'd be able to with anyone. He'd married her! He'd given her that blasted ring and taken her to bed. He'd let her in, let himself hope, believe that he could have the future he'd dreamed of. That he was enough for her…and now? Now she said she couldn't sign.

No. That wasn't the way this plan went at all.

He thumped his fist against the wood of the bridal suite door, but didn't wait for her to tell him to come in. She had to know he'd follow, had to know he'd need an explanation.

'Flynn, I…I'm sorry.' She looked so small curled up on the bed, her knees under her chin and her arms wrapped tightly around them.

'Then come downstairs and sign the agreement.' Maybe this was just last-minute nerves. Some fear of paperwork he didn't fully understand.

But Helena shook her head. 'I can't. I'm sorry.'

'I don't want apologies. I want reasons.' He hadn't even moved from the doorway, he realised. There was no point staying if she wouldn't explain. He wasn't sure, but he thought his grip on the door handle might be the only thing keeping him upright while he waited for her answer.

'I can't sign it because it's not true. The declarations.'

Flynn blinked at her, his mind foggy with incomprehension. 'What? You're already married?' She shook her head. 'You're in love with someone else?' Both sisters? Surely that was too cruel a joke for the universe to play, even on him.

'No. Not that.' Her words came out almost as a croak. As if her throat didn't want to let them leave.

And then her meaning sank in, and he wished he'd never heard her at all.

'You have a child.' There was no emotion in his voice, he realised, because it was all swirling inside him. Every possible negative feeling—betrayal, horror, pain and everything in between—ran through his blood, his muscles, his organs, causing them to seize up and scream in silent pain. 'Where is it now?'

It. He'd married the woman and he didn't know she had a child—and even now he could only call the poor thing 'it' because he didn't know enough to know if it was a girl or a boy.

'She was adopted,' Helena whispered, and every single drop of those awful emotions prepared to come tumbling out of him.

'You gave her away.' He couldn't look away, couldn't focus on anything except her face. He'd thought that she'd let him in, thought they were planning a life together. When all the time she'd been holding back, keeping him at a distance as he'd tumbled headfirst into love with her. His plan wasn't hers, and never would be.

'It was a mistake. I was sixteen and I was so, so scared.' Her words were tumbling out over each other, but he was barely listening. He was still trying to make sense of this horrific reality he now found himself in. One where the woman he loved was a woman who lied, who left people behind. And to think he'd believed her when she'd promised she'd stay, that they could have a life together. He was an idiot. After thirty long years, didn't he know better than to believe any person who said they'd take him into their heart, love him and keep him as their own?

'When I told Thea—'

'Thea knew.' Of course Thea knew. Who else would Helena turn to? And why would Thea mention it to him? She could never have imagined that Helena would jump into her place so fast. No, he couldn't blame Thea for this one. Only Helena. 'Who else?'

'Um…my father. And Isabella.' Not his father, of course. If Ezekiel had known, this would have come up sooner, the moment the old man had realised they were married. He'd have rubbed this in just to cause Flynn pain.

But Thomas. Thomas had known and he'd

stood there and nodded when Flynn explained that he and Helena were getting married. Had laughed when Ezekiel talked about Flynn getting Helena pregnant—and had never mentioned that he wouldn't be the first.

'They sent me away,' Helena said, those blue-bell eyes still wide but somehow no longer so innocent. 'As soon as they found out they got me out of town, somewhere I couldn't be a scandal or a bother.' She sounded so broken, so distraught, he almost wanted to take her in his arms and comfort her. But he knew that he was still seeing her as *his* Helena. And she wasn't any more. She was a stranger, one who'd lied about who she was, what she could be to him. What he could be to her.

If she'd truly loved him, if she'd really wanted their future together, she'd have told him about her baby. And if she'd told him before he fell...at least he could have discussed it rationally, seen if there was still a chance for them to make this work. Maybe not with all the hearts, flowers and romance they'd hoped for, but a pragmatic business marriage as originally planned.

But she'd let him fall in love with her then torn his heart out by telling him that his whole image of her was a lie. That she wasn't the person she'd promised to be.

He'd told her everything—how it had felt,

growing up as the spare part in the Ashton household, knowing he wasn't wanted or needed any more, once his parents had Zeke. She must have known exactly what it would do to him, knowing that she'd done that to her own child—given it away to an uncertain fate. And she'd kept it from him until it was too late.

Until he loved her.

It was calculated, cruel, and the Helena he'd fallen for would never have done it. That was what he needed to remember. The Helena he loved didn't really exist. Instead, all he was left with was a wife he barely knew and would never, ever understand.

'This is what your father meant, isn't it? When he said you were making up for past mistakes.' Flynn lowered his head and laughed, all bitterness and no humour. 'What? You think marrying one poor adopted boy makes up for the girl you gave away without a second thought?'

'No! Of course I don't. You don't understand—'

'You're right—I don't understand!' Flynn roared, tearing himself away from the door as he strode across to the bed when she sat. He wouldn't touch her—couldn't bring himself to—but he wasn't going to keep a safe distance either. Helena scooted up to cower against the headboard anyway. Another sign she'd never known him at all.

'I don't understand how you could have sat there at lunch yesterday and listened to me telling you how I wasn't wanted—by my birth parents or my adoptive ones—and promised to make a better life, a better family with me, when all along you were no better than any of them.' The shame of the secrets and feelings he'd admitted to this woman burned. Maybe she hadn't been laughing at him all along, but she'd still let him spill his guts while she gave up nothing at all.

She'd still lied to him about the person she was.

'I thought I knew you. Thought we knew each other,' he said. 'But the woman I bought that ring for could never give away her own child.'

Helena's face paled, spots of bright red blazing on her cheekbones in contrast. Tearing her engagement ring from her finger, she threw it across the bed towards him. It clattered off the edge and on to the floorboards, but he made no move to retrieve it. What would he do with such a thing now, anyway?

'You thought you knew me? All because you could pick out a ring I liked?' Helena hurled the words at him as if he were in the wrong. As if she had any grounds to argue at all.

'Because I thought we'd been open and honest with each other!' Gripping the end of the bed frame, Flynn tried not to remember how close he'd felt to her, here in this very room.

Helena shook her head, her blonde hair curling wildly in the air. 'No. You thought you'd found someone who fitted your plan, your schedule. You thought you could make me the wife you needed. You married me for my name, remember, nothing more. I was just your convenient stand-in bride.'

'You know that's not all you were.' If that were so, why would it hurt so much now to know the truth?

'Wasn't I? Then why were you so desperate for me to sign my life away to you?'

'I wanted a future with you! A family!' He was shouting, he knew it, knew everyone in the house must be able to hear them. He didn't care. Not any more.

'But you never asked me if that was what I wanted!' Helena yelled back, up on her knees now as she faced him. 'You say you wanted a family, but all you really wanted was an heir. Something to legitimise you as a real Ashton, to give you full control of the company. Why else were you so set on marrying Thea? And why did you marry me with no contract, no agreement?'

'Don't you dare.' Cold fury ran through him like a wave. 'You think you can tell me why I wanted a child of my own? You, of all people?

Who had that and just gave it away. Gave her away. You called her a *mistake*.'

Helena reared back as if he'd slapped her. 'You have no idea what you're talking about.'

'Oh, I think I do,' Flynn answered. 'I imagine it went something like this. Poor little rich girl, doesn't get as much notice as her clever older sister. Wants Daddy to pay her some attention too so she starts acting out—the usual teenage rebellion. Dates inappropriate boys, stays out partying—all the classics. But one day she goes too far, realises she's pregnant. Maybe you didn't even know who the father was.' She flinched at that, and he knew he'd hit a nerve. Part of him took a vicious pleasure in the fact. 'So you go crying to big sis, make her tell Daddy for you. And Daddy fixes everything, right? Sends you away to have the baby then palms it off to somebody else—no harm, no foul. No damage done—except to that poor kid's life.'

She jerked back at his words, as if they caused physical pain.

Good. He wanted her to hurt. Wanted her to feel the same pain he did.

If he couldn't love her any more, he had to break things between them altogether. Their marriage would never be anything more than a convenience, from this day forward.

It was all over for them now. It had to be.

* * *

Helena stared at him, horrified. How could this be the same man she'd shared this bed with the night before? Or even the man she'd worshipped at fourteen for his kind understanding? This Flynn was someone she barely recognised. 'You're right. You don't know me at all.' No more than she knew him, apparently.

'On the contrary, I believe I've finally got a glimpse of the real you.' Flynn's mouth twisted in a cruel sneer. 'And the sight sickens me.'

He didn't know, Helena told herself. He didn't know the truth of what had happened to her that night. But he wouldn't listen either. Just like her father never had.

She couldn't forgive him for that.

'Trust me, the feeling is mutual.'

'What did you expect, Helena?' Flynn threw his arms wide, the injured party, hurt and wounded at her hand. And he was, she knew. She should have told him the truth from the start, let him make his own choice with all the information. But things had moved so fast, and she couldn't bear the thought of losing him so soon after he'd finally become hers. She'd wanted them to build a relationship that could survive the truth.

Great job, Helena.

'Did you think you could keep it a secret forever?' Flynn asked. 'Or at least make me fall so in love with you that it wouldn't matter what horrific things you'd done in your past?'

She felt the colour rise in her cheeks, warm and humiliating. That was, of course, exactly what she'd thought. Or hoped, at least.

She should have known better. People didn't ever really forgive, not when it mattered. Even taking her sister's place and marrying Flynn hadn't been enough for their father to forgive either of them. Why should Flynn be any different?

'I thought you'd respect me enough to listen to me when I told you. To hear my reasons and try to understand.'

'You want me to listen? I'll listen. Tell me, Helena. How did it feel to give away your own child to a total stranger? Did you feel bad for a whole day, or just until your daddy gave you your credit card back so you could go shoe shopping?'

He didn't have a clue. Didn't know her or care for her enough to give her the benefit of the doubt, even.

'It's all black and white to you, isn't it?' she said, staring at the man she'd thought she loved. 'On-plan or off-schedule. Right or wrong. Us and them. It doesn't occur to you that people might have reasons or beliefs or feelings different to yours, does it? You can't imagine any scenario in which I might have done the right thing.'

'The right thing? How can giving away a child

ever be the right thing?' Flynn stood gripping the frame at the foot of the bed, his arms stretched out to the sides as he loomed over her. Helena swallowed, her mouth dry as the image of him there, so much stronger and more powerful than her, took her back to another awful day. The worst of her life from the day her mother died until now.

Two other men, barely more than boys, that same look in their eyes. The look that told her she didn't matter to them, that what she wanted, the decisions she made, didn't matter at all. She meant nothing.

She had put herself there in that room with them. She'd made her choice and now she would pay for it.

'You can't tell me you thought you were giving her a better life,' Flynn went on, and Helena flinched at just the accusation in his voice. 'You come from one of the richest families in the country. You could have given that child everything it ever needed and you chose not to.'

'No.' It wasn't loud, but Helena put every bit of feeling she had behind the word. 'No, I couldn't. I couldn't give her what she needed most.'

'And what was that?' Flynn asked, a bitter mocking tone in his voice.

'Love.' She looked up and met his eyes then, took every glimmer of hatred and disgust he had to give. 'I couldn't have loved her the way she needed, the way she deserved. And so I agreed when they told me I had to give her away.'

'You couldn't...' Flynn shook his head in disbelief. 'You really are a piece of work, aren't you? Have you honestly convinced yourself that you did what was best for that child?'

'You tell me.' Helena got up from the bed. She needed to be equal with him for this, couldn't let him glare down at her any more. He still had almost a foot of height on her, but at least she didn't feel quite so helpless. She fisted her hands at her hips and stared him down. 'You grew up in a family like mine—our families were practically one and the same for years. You tell me, how did it feel to grow up there without being wanted or loved? Because if it felt anything like my childhood did after my mother died, you wouldn't wish it on anyone.'

For a moment he looked stunned, and she wondered if this was her opportunity. Her one chance to make him truly understand what had happened that night and how it had changed her. How knowing it was all her own fault had only made everything that followed a thousand times harder.

Could she make him understand the depths of despair she'd hit? How it had felt as if her soul had been torn apart the moment she'd realised she could never look at or think of her own child without remembering the night that she had been conceived? Without feeling that same pain over and over again?

But then his expression changed and the repulsion in his eyes grew greater than ever.

'If that's truly how you feel, Helena, perhaps you should ask yourself something. How are you any different from your father or, worse, mine? And what kind of *monster* can't love their own child?'

Monster.

The word hit her in the gut and she wrapped her arms around herself as she doubled over, as if he'd hit her with bullets not insults. He was right. He didn't understand and he wouldn't listen, but he was still right.

But if he thought she could ever forgive herself for the decisions she'd made, then he hadn't got a clue about her.

'Do you think I don't live with that knowledge every day?' she asked. 'Why do you think I held out against the agreement? I know you want kids and I know I can't have them. We could have adopted, perhaps, but the thought of carrying another child...I couldn't do it. Even for you.'

'Do you think I'd want you to, now? Do you think I can even imagine touching you?' Revulsion shadowed his face. 'You say you live with it every day. Well, so will I, now. Because you talked me into marrying you, into *sleeping with you,* and now we're stuck with each other.'

'You want a divorce?' Helena asked. 'I'll give you one, and gladly. We can both be free. You can find another way to find that legitimacy you crave. Except there isn't one, is there? You've run out of Morrison sisters now. It's me and my sordid past or nothing at all. Entirely up to you.'

Hatred burned from Flynn's eyes, and Helena realised that they could be making each other unhappy for the rest of their lives. That knowing how happy they could have been would only make their misery more bitter.

Maybe this was her punishment, at last. Or her atonement.

Either way, she thanked God no children would have to live through it with them.

The air between them crackled with anger, frustration and helplessness, and Helena couldn't look away from him if she tried. She needed to know. Would he choose this hell of a relationship, just to keep the company? Or would he walk away with his integrity intact?

But she didn't find out. Because, just then, Henry knocked on the open door.

'I hate to interrupt,' he said in a tone that said he was glad to have a reason to separate them right now. 'But I just had a call from London. I'm so sorry, Helena, but your father has been rushed to hospital. Heart attack. We need to get back to London. Immediately.'

CHAPTER TEN

HELENA KEPT HER silence all the way to London.

She felt as if she'd spoken all the words inside of her already; that if she tried for any more all that would come out would be gibberish. She had no more angry barbs to throw at Flynn, no more defences to try, no more arguments to make. And she was still too far from understanding what her father's heart attack meant, or how she felt about it, to even begin to speak on the subject.

So she grabbed her most important things in silence, forcing them into her carry-on bag, knowing that the villa staff would pack up and send on the rest. She dressed as comfortably and casually as she could manage, needing the sensation of soft cotton and warm cashmere against her skin, now she couldn't rely on her husband's touch.

She slipped her sunglasses on, nodded goodbye to the maid at the door and climbed into the back of the car Henry had hired at the airport, ignoring the two men in the front.

And then she headed home.

It was dark by the time they reached the hospital. Henry had asked—not Flynn, of course; he'd barely looked at her for the last thousand miles—if she wanted to go home first, to change, to sleep, whatever. But Helena had shaken her head, and he'd asked the taxi driver to go straight to the hospital.

Drizzle misted the windows of the cab, familiar, damp and chill. Suddenly, Helena was glad to be back home. Tuscany had felt like such an escape, such a fairy tale, until today. But she knew it could never be that for her again. And to stay another moment would only ever have reminded her of what she'd lost.

She didn't wait for Henry or Flynn to follow as she strode into the hospital. Flynn had called his mother from the car and Helena had heard enough to know where her father was, so she headed straight to him.

Isabella seemed to have aged a decade in just a week. She stood, leaning against the wall outside Thomas's room, her make-up faded and her hair no longer fixed in place. She looked up as Helena approached and her face crumpled.

'Is he…?' Her first words for a thousand miles, Helena thought, and she couldn't even finish the sentence.

Isabella shook her head. 'The doctors say the surgery went well. They've done…' she gulped in air and Helena realised she was trying to keep from crying; Isabella, the icy matriarch, had actual tears in her eyes '…something,' she finished. 'They'll tell you all about it. I don't…I don't understand it all. Not at all.'

It was the day for it, Helena thought. Nothing at all made sense today.

Flynn and Henry caught up at last, Flynn wrapping his arms around his mother in a way Helena was sure she'd never done for him. Did he know, she wondered, about Isabella and Thomas's decade-long affair? She'd never asked. One more secret between them, she supposed.

Ignored, Helena moved to the door, pushing it open to step inside her father's room. He looked smaller there in the bed, hooked up to machines and tucked under crisp white hospital sheets. He wouldn't even know she was there. And if he didn't recover, if something else happened…he might never know how her past had come back to screw up her present. That he'd been right that night eight years ago when he'd told her she'd wilfully ruined her life.

'Oh, Daddy.' Her throat thickened as the tears welled up. Clenching her fists, Helena tried to stop them, tried to keep at bay all the feelings that threatened to wash her away in their flood.

'Helena?' Henry's cautious voice came from behind her, but she didn't turn. 'Are you okay? Do you need…anything?'

No, she wasn't okay. She might never be okay again. She hurt so deep she thought her bones might crack, and she feared that anger might be the only thing holding her together—anger at her father for almost dying, at Flynn for not understanding, at those not quite men who had almost destroyed her, and at herself for letting them.

Henry couldn't fix any of that. But there was one thing he might be able to do.

'I need my sister,' she told him.

It took an hour of persuasion to get his mother to leave the hospital and, even then, she wouldn't go home. Instead, Isabella insisted on being taken to Thomas's town house, saying she wouldn't be able to sleep anywhere else.

Flynn supposed this meant that the polite charade of ignoring the fact that his mother had been sleeping with his father's best friend for the last ten years was over. Everybody's secrets were being exposed today, and it left Flynn feeling as if he'd been scraped raw.

Helena wouldn't leave her father's room, and Flynn had refused to even try to persuade *her*.

Henry waited for him in the cab while he got his mother settled, then asked, 'Where to now?' as soon as he returned.

Flynn wished he had an answer. A bar was tempting—somewhere he could drink away the memory of the last week. But when he sobered up nothing would have changed, and a hangover wouldn't help anything at all.

He wasn't facing his father tonight, not while his mother was sleeping at another man's house. So that left him with the house he'd had prepared for himself and his wife to come home to after their honeymoon. It probably wasn't even fully furnished yet but it was *his* and Henry had the keys.

'Let's go to the town house. See if they've delivered the liquor cabinet yet.' Because, while a night of whisky in some dive bar was off the cards, there was no way he was getting to sleep without a drink tonight.

Henry gave the address to the driver and Flynn tipped his head back against the headrest and tried not to think until they arrived there.

The house loomed out of the darkness like a mausoleum. Flynn forced images of how he'd imagined his life in this place from his mind as Henry fumbled with the keys, and made his way straight to the library as soon as the door swung open. Boxes of books sat unopened on the floor, surrounded by empty shelves awaiting them. His desk had been placed at the wrong angle in the corner, but next to it sat his liquor cabinet. It was empty, of course, but a short search turned up the box containing his collection of fine malts and Henry soon tracked down the tumblers in the kitchen.

Flynn pulled the two wing chairs into position on opposite sides of the empty fireplace, ignored the mess around them and poured them each a double measure of his favourite Scotch.

Henry waited until his whisky was halfway down the glass before he spoke, which Flynn appreciated.

'So. What happens now?'

The question he'd been avoiding all night. 'I have no idea.'

'Okay. Well, I guess you don't need to figure it all out tonight. You both need time, and with her father sick... Helena's asked me to find Thea. Get her home.'

Flynn looked up at his friend, noting that the concern in his voice was echoed in his expression. 'How much did you hear? Earlier.'

'Enough.' Henry's voice rang heavy and he stared into his glass.

'I can't...I can't comprehend any of it right now.'

'The reasons you wanted this marriage—enough to marry the wrong sister, even. They haven't gone away.' He was playing devil's advocate now, Flynn knew. The consummate solicitor, Henry always could make both sides of any argument.

'I know.'

Henry sighed. 'I'll leave you the agreement anyway—the draft version. Read it through again. Maybe it'll help you come to a decision.' He pulled the thick stack of paper from his laptop bag and placed it on Flynn's desk. 'I'd better go. I'll call tomorrow, see how things are.'

Flynn nodded, more to show that he'd heard him than in agreement.

'And, Flynn?' Henry said from the door. 'Try to sleep, yeah?'

He didn't even bother nodding that time. Instead, he sat and stared at the contract that was supposed to ensure his future, his family. He sipped his Scotch and when it was gone he poured himself another.

When he finished that one, he stood, grabbed the stack of paper and tossed it in the empty fireplace.

It could be the first thing to burn when he unpacked the matches.

CHAPTER ELEVEN

HELENA HADN'T WANTED to go home—not least because she wasn't entirely sure where home was. But by mid-morning the next day, after Helena had spent the night sleeping in a very uncomfortable armchair next to her dad's bed, Isabella was back, looking well rested, immaculate but still with an edge of fear in her eyes.

'Helena, darling, go home and take a shower. Flynn will be waiting for you—you haven't even seen your new marital home yet!'

'I'm fine here, really,' Helena said, wishing she couldn't feel the creases on her face where she'd fallen asleep against a striped cushion. 'Besides, all my stuff is still at Dad's house.' That was a thought. Maybe she could just nip back there long enough to shower and change, now she wouldn't have to share the space with Isabella.

'No, it isn't.' Isabella laid down the words like a trump card. 'I had everything packed up and moved over to the town house the moment we returned from Italy. All your clothes, books, personal belongings—they're all there waiting for you in your new home.'

Along with a husband who couldn't bear to look at her. Perfect.

'I want to wait until Dad wakes up.'

Isabella's expression grew concerned again, and she turned to tug Thomas's sheet a little higher over his chest. 'Shouldn't he have woken up already? The doctors don't seem concerned, but even here I don't feel you ever really have one-on-one attention, do you?'

'They're taking good care of him.' Helena tried to sound soothing, and also tried to forget that she was talking to her father's married lover. 'The best care. And they say he shouldn't wake up until this evening, so—'

'So you have plenty of time to go home, shower and see your husband,' Isabella finished for her, leaving Helena to realise, too late, that she'd been outmanoeuvred by her mother-in-law.

She spent the cab ride to the town house rehearsing what she'd say to Flynn in her head, but it proved unnecessary. Whether he'd gone to the office or his parents' house, or even back to Italy, Helena had no idea, but Flynn was not home. Not in their home.

She wandered the half unpacked rooms, filled with unfamiliar possessions, taking in the trappings of what should have been her future. In what she assumed was supposed to be the library she found two empty crystal tumblers and a bottle of Scotch—the only real evidence so far that Flynn had even been there at all.

She dropped into one of the chairs, bone-weary, and wondered if this was where he'd sat the night before. Wondered if he'd ever speak to her again, if she'd ever get the chance to explain herself. If it would even make a difference.

She frowned, squinting at the fireplace in front of her. What was that? Leaning forward, she fished out the papers and immediately wished that she hadn't.

As she flicked through the pages of what should have been her post-nuptial agreement, Flynn's plan for their future, she felt the tears begin to fall at last, hot and thick against her cheeks. And, as the words blurred in front of her, she began to rewrite them in her mind, to imagine them the way they should be.

A future she'd want to live. Not one based around who got what or a schedule they had to follow. But a future that grew organically, from the love between two people.

She didn't want a piece of paper compelling her to live her life bullet point by bullet point. And if Flynn thought that was what he needed…he was wrong. He'd spent his whole life so far trying to place order on an existence that had started in chaos—with not belonging, with bad timing, with uncertainty and manipulation. But he couldn't do that forever. Life didn't work that way.

She only had to look at her father in his hospital bed to know that.

Or think about the moment she'd crossed out her sister's name on that wedding invitation.

Life leapt out at you when you least expected it, and all you could do was hold on for the ride. And someone needed to teach Flynn Ashton that fact.

Maybe even her.

Wiping her tears away with the back of her hand, Helena reached into her handbag and pulled out a pen. Deliberately, and with several thick black lines, she crossed out the boring legalese title and replaced it with her own.

A Manifesto for a More Spontaneous Marriage.

She smiled at the words for a moment, her mind suddenly filled with ideas and possibilities and a world of impulsive romance. Of amazed joy.

And then, starting on the back of page one, she began to write out every hope and dream she had for her future.

Even if she had to accept it would never have Flynn in it.

* * *

Flynn couldn't stay in the house so he went to the only place he really ever felt at home. The office.

He arrived while the place was still abandoned and dark, even the most conscientious employees still tucked up in their beds. He turned on his computer, settled back in his chair and lost himself in emails and memos and contracts for as long as he could.

By the time the sun was fully up, he'd caught up on everything that had happened since he'd left for Italy. He almost wished he hadn't spent so much time keeping on top of his emails when he was away—it would have given him more of a distraction now, when he needed it.

And more time to spend with Helena, before everything he'd thought they were building together came crashing down.

'So, you made it back.' His father's creaky voice jerked Flynn out of his own dark thoughts. He looked up to see the old man standing in his doorway, staring down at him the same way he'd always done when Flynn's school reports came in, however good they were. 'I heard tell you'd cut short your honeymoon. I assume you got your wife to sign the papers, as we discussed?'

Of course, that was all he was concerned about. His best friend and business partner was in hospital, his own wife hadn't left the man's side, but all Ezekiel Ashton cared about was paperwork.

Exactly what Helena had accused Flynn of.

'Helena's father just suffered a massive heart attack. Last I heard, he still hadn't woken up. Forgive me for not pressing her on the formalities just yet.' His voice sounded icy-cold, even to his own ears, but Flynn wondered how much he was speaking to his father and how much to himself. He wanted this sorted as much as the old man did.

He wanted it finished so he could move past the ache that never seemed to leave his chest.

'I understand that Thomas has the only woman he needs dancing attendance on him already.' There was bitterness in Ezekiel's voice, deeper than Flynn had heard from him before. 'I'm sure his daughter is superfluous to the proceedings.'

'She's in love with him, you know. Mum, I mean.' Flynn didn't say it to wound. Just to see if his father would react. If he could even feign surprise this late in the game.

'Of course she is,' Ezekiel scoffed. 'Any fool could see that for the last ten years or more. But she never left me, did she? She always knew I could give her more.'

Flynn thought about his mother's face, careworn in a way he'd never seen it as she'd brushed her hand against Thomas's cheek. 'She might now, I think.'

'Then she's more of a fool than your brother and your runaway bride put together.'

'Actually,' Flynn said, 'I'm starting to think that Thea and Zeke were the only ones to get things right in all this.'

Ezekiel's blank expression told Flynn all he needed to know. His father would never understand love—not the way that Flynn hoped to understand it one day.

'Get that post-nuptial agreement to me by the end of the week,' Ezekiel said before turning and walking away.

Flynn stared after him long after he had gone. Whatever happened next with him and Helena, it wouldn't be about paperwork, not any more. It wouldn't be a schedule or a plan.

He couldn't love a woman who couldn't love her own child; it was as simple and as hard as that. Couldn't trust a woman who had lied, and left a helpless baby behind, not to do the same to him when it suited her. And no amount of planning or paperwork could change that.

Helena awoke from dozing in her chair at the sound of a phone ringing. It took a moment for her to identify it as hers, and longer to find and answer it.

'Helena? It's Henry. I wanted to let you know

that I got hold of your sister. She'll meet you at the hospital as soon as her flight gets in tonight.'

'I'll be there.' She wiped the sleep from her eyes and tried to focus. 'Thanks, Henry.'

Dropping the phone into her lap, she stretched her arms up above her head, trying to relieve the ache in her shoulders. It was almost six; Flynn would be home before too long, she assumed, and she wanted to be out of the way again before that happened.

She bit her lip and stared at the mass of paper in her lap, no longer neatly clipped together and numbered, but loose and covered in her messy scrawl that grew less intelligible by the word. It would probably never make sense to another person, and she wasn't even sure she could take it with her and look at it every day without remembering the day she hadn't signed it. But she'd written it, and somehow that felt like enough.

Leaving the agreement on Flynn's desk, Helena grabbed a few of her things, packing a bag with some changes of clothes and the basic necessities. She'd need to come back sooner rather than later, but it would see her through the next day at least. Isabella might have moved her stuff here, but Helena knew she couldn't stay. She'd figure something else out.

So, with only a brief glance back at the manifesto she'd written, Helena Ashton straightened her hair and clothes and silently slipped out of the house that should have been her home.

It was time to move on.

The hospital room looked almost exactly as she had left it. Thomas still lay peacefully sleeping, the heart monitor beeping at his side, and Isabella sat in the armchair beside him, pretending to read a magazine. Helena thought she might still be on the same page she'd been staring at that morning.

'No change?' she asked from the door, and Isabella's head jerked up at the sound of her voice.

'He woke up earlier. Not for very long. But he seemed himself. He…was glad I was here.' The relief in Isabella's voice was palpable and Helena felt the knot in her middle start to loosen, just a touch.

'That's great. That's…wonderful.' Helena sank down into the other, less comfortable chair in the room. She might not be sure how she felt about her father right now—beyond furious and hurt—but she wasn't ready to lose the only parent she had left. Not yet. And not before she'd figured out what to make of her relationship with him.

'Henry called earlier,' Helena said, smoothing down the edge of Thomas's sheets, even though they didn't need it. 'Thea's on her way—presumably with Zeke; I didn't ask. She'll be here tonight.'

Isabella froze, the lines of her shoulders and neck suddenly sharp. 'I must admit, I didn't expect to see them again so soon.'

'I imagine they feel the same.'

Helena had assumed that everyone would have had time to get over the wedding fallout before they were all together again. That she and Flynn would be happily living their lives and Thea's runaway bride act could become a near-miss, a funny story to tell at dinner parties. *Can you believe how wrong we nearly got this? Thea almost married Flynn! Isn't that crazy?*

But not now. Now, those conversations would go very differently indeed. And Helena had been so preoccupied with the idea of having her big sister here, where she belonged, where she needed her, that she hadn't even thought about what she was going to say. How she was going to explain what had happened since she'd left.

Or how other people would feel to see her.

Their father had been furiously disappointed in Thea. But surely that would change now? Now that he was lying in a hospital bed with an uncertain future, of course he'd want both his daughters there.

Helena had to believe that or there was no hope for her family at all.

'I'm going to get coffee,' Helena said. 'Do you want coffee?'

Isabella nodded, but her eyes were already fixed on Thomas's face again.

Three cups of coffee later, Thea arrived in a flurry of activity, sweeping through the hospital as if she were back in her power suit and high heels instead of the floaty sundress she was actually wearing. Zeke followed in her wake, grim-faced and suitcase in hand.

Their father was sleeping again, so Thea quizzed his doctors more thoroughly than Isabella or Helena had managed. Helena waited outside while Zeke spoke with his mother and Thea asked more questions.

Then they stepped out of the room again and Helena felt the weight on her shoulders start to lift.

'You're here.' Helena stared at her sister across the hospital corridor. 'You came.' And then she burst into tears.

'Okay, so I was gone less than a week,' Thea said, putting her arm around Helena's shoulders. Helena resisted the urge to snuggle up to her like a toddler, but only just. 'Explain to me exactly how everything went up in smoke in my absence?'

'Firstly, it is not my fault that Dad had a heart attack,' Helena said. 'Or that Isabella appears to have left Ezekiel and moved into Dad's house.'

Thea blinked. 'Okay, well, that's a start. What is your fault, then?'

This was the big one. Helena almost wished she didn't have to tell her. Thea looked so relaxed, so happy—and at least five years younger. It was amazing what love could do, Helena thought, as Zeke brought over more coffee and a couple of plates of sandwiches. The hospital dining area was nicer than Helena had imagined it would be, even in a private hospital. Too nice, in fact, for the scene she was pretty sure it was about to witness.

She took a breath.

'I married Flynn.'

'You what?' Zeke swore as he spilt boiling coffee over his hand. 'Give a guy some warning for that kind of news, will you?'

'Sorry.' Helena flashed him a quick smile then turned her attention back to Thea.

Her sister's eyes were wide and disbelieving. 'Why? Did Dad make you? Or Isabella?'

'It was my idea,' Helena told her. 'All mine. After you left, when I thought about actually having to go down there and tell everyone the wedding was off, this seemed like a better option.' It sounded stupid out loud, Helena thought.

'A…better option? After you spent weeks—months!—telling me to get out, that I couldn't marry someone I didn't love.' Thea sounded outraged at the very idea.

'I know. I know. But it was different for me.'

'Different—how?' Zeke asked, frowning. But Thea's eyes had gone wide and sad, and she touched her fingertips to her lips as she said, 'Oh, Helena. You loved him.'

Helena shook her head. 'Not at the start. It wasn't that simple. I mean, maybe I never got over that crush I had when I was fourteen, not totally, but I wasn't planning on basing a marriage on that. I thought, since there was no contract, we could just get a quiet little divorce once the scandal died down. I knew he wanted kids and I…can't think about that. So I knew it couldn't work out. But then…he convinced me it could be more. That we could have a future together, have everything he was supposed to have with you.'

'Want me to kill him?' Zeke asked Thea conversationally. 'I gave that man everything he wanted—the company, mostly, admittedly—and he took Helena too. I can kill him.'

'I'd…rather you didn't,' Helena said. 'Even after everything.'

'Tell me about "everything",' Thea instructed. 'And, Zeke, stop interrupting.'

'I don't even know how to describe it. I can't say what changed. We talked a lot. I learned a lot—about him, about how he grew up. He bought me a ring.' Her gaze jumped down to her left hand, where only the too tight wedding band remained. 'I fell in love.'

'So what went wrong?' Thea asked. 'Because, given that this all happened over the course of the last week and you've been crying pretty much constantly since I arrived, I'm figuring it has to be big. Tell me, so I can fix it.'

Helena gave her a watery smile. 'You can't fix this one, Thea.'

'Watch me try.'

'I couldn't sign the post-nuptial agreement Henry brought over. It had a line in it...I had to swear that I had no children.'

'Oh.' Thea's eyes closed as she listened.

'So I had to tell him about...' Helena swallowed. 'I told him I was sixteen, I had a baby and I gave her away.'

'What did he say?' Zeke asked, his voice tense.

'He called me a monster.' Helena shrugged. She figured that covered the basics.

'Okay, now I really am going to kill him.' Zeke was on his feet before Thea grabbed his arm and pulled him back down.

'Did you explain? What happened to you?' Thea's gaze focused so tightly on Helena's face that she squirmed under the attention.

'I didn't get into details, no.' Helena sighed. 'I don't think it would make any difference, anyway.'

'If he knew you were raped?' Zeke shook his head. 'You're wrong. My brother might be an idiot but…it makes a difference.'

'Does it really?' Helena wasn't sure if she was asking them or herself. 'I put myself in that position. I went there, I got drunk and they told me I said yes. And I know, in my head, that they were wrong—that they abused me and they committed a crime. I know that, I do. But…'

'But?' Thea pressed when Helena stopped.

'But I was the one who couldn't love that child, no matter how she came into the world. And that's what I know he'll never forgive me for.'

The tears came again then. Thea wrapped her arms around her, and Helena clung to her big sister like a lifeline.

Thea couldn't fix this one, she knew. But maybe having her there would be enough to help her through it.

'You need to tell him, sweetheart,' Thea murmured against her hair. 'He deserves to know everything.'

'I know,' Helena whispered back. Because not telling Flynn everything had got her into this mess. And maybe it wouldn't make a difference—maybe she didn't even want it to. But if she ever wanted to move past this, she had to get it all out.

And then leave it behind.

'I'll go with you,' Zeke said. 'We can pick up the rest of your stuff while we're there.'

Helena nodded, grateful to have someone else making the decisions for a while.

'You can do this.' Thea tucked a finger under Helena's chin, making her look up into her eyes. 'And I will be right here for you, every step of the way.'

Helena gave another shaky nod. Thea was right.

She'd survived worse than this, with her sister beside her. And she'd survive it again.

She turned to Zeke. 'Then let's go and get this over with.'

CHAPTER TWELVE

FLYNN IGNORED THE knock on the door the first time. He'd already spoken to Henry at the office, dealt with his father and phoned his mother. Anyone else could go jump as far as he was concerned.

But, by the third knock, even Flynn had to admit that whoever it was didn't seem to be going away.

He wrenched the door open and found he couldn't even muster up any surprise at seeing his brother on his doorstep—or Helena standing just behind him.

'We've come for Helena's things.' Zeke glanced at Helena, who seemed to shrink back further, then turned back to Flynn, his jaw set and eyes full of fury. 'And while she's packing, you and I are going to have a word.'

The anger that had never been more than a moment away, ever since Thea and Zeke had left, simmered up closer to the surface. 'I suppose that's logical. You run off with my fiancée on my wedding day, and you think now is the time to talk.'

Zeke stepped inside and from the corner of his eye Flynn saw Helena slip in behind him, heading for the staircase. He wanted to stare, to take her in one last time, but he wouldn't let himself. He had to cut her out of his life completely. It was *good* that she'd come for her things.

'Nothing about this situation is logical. Flynn—' Zeke started, but Flynn couldn't let him finish.

'So what? You don't like the mess you left behind so you're here to whisk Helena away too? What's wrong with you? Is one sister really not enough?'

He felt the punch before he saw it, the blossoming throb of pain radiating from his cheekbone as Zeke pulled his fist back. The surge of adrenalin had him wanting to return it, to break his brother's face for coming here after everything that had happened, for acting so righteous. His hands balled up into weapons as he prepared to strike—

Until a small hand grabbed his arm and yanked it back.

'Stop it. Both of you. Idiots!' Helena's cheeks had spots of red in them as she glared at them both. 'Zeke, I thought you were coming here to support me?'

'And I thought you were going to do the talking,' Zeke countered.

Helena's jaw tightened and Flynn couldn't help but wonder what it was she still had to say. How could there be anything left?

'Fine.' She grabbed a bag from behind her and thrust it into Zeke's hands. 'In that case, you go and pack. We'll be in here when you're finished.' She jerked her head towards the door of the library.

Inside, Helena seemed perfectly at home in a room he hadn't even realised she knew existed. With decisive strides, she made her way to the desk and, grabbing two tumblers, poured them both a whisky. Turning, she handed one to Flynn and he could see the uncertainty in her eyes, even as she ran the show.

She thought he would reject her again, even though she'd sent Zeke upstairs to pack so she could leave him, once and for all. How many more ways were there for them to show each other they weren't meant to be?

'Okay, look, this is what's going to happen here,' Helena said, clutching her own glass with both hands as she sat down in the chair nearest the desk. Raising his eyebrows, Flynn followed suit, settling into his own chair. 'I am going to tell you some things. Not because I think you deserve to hear them, and not because I think they'll change anything.'

'Then why are you bothering?' Flynn asked because he had to try and remember which Helena this was now. It was just harder with her sitting right there, blonde and lovely and tired and hurt.

'Because it matters to me. Because I need to have the full truth out there before I can move on.' She gave a light shrug. 'And because Thea told me to.'

'Then by all means,' Flynn said with excessive courtesy, 'talk away.' It wouldn't make any difference. It couldn't, not now.

Helena sucked in a breath then paused as if she hadn't expected the permission to be granted so easily. She took a sip of whisky before she started to talk.

'When I was sixteen, I snuck out of the house to meet an older boy, one I knew I wasn't supposed to see. He took me over to his friend's house, said we'd have a little party.'

Flynn shifted in his seat. He didn't want to hear this, didn't need to hear this. 'And you were all about the parties, right?'

Helena ignored him. 'When I got there, they gave me a drink, then another one. And another—maybe more. I wasn't used to alcohol so it affected me quickly. But I wasn't so drunk that I didn't tell them to stop when they tried to take my top off. I wasn't so far gone that I didn't scream when they raped me, one after another. I knew they were lying when they said afterwards that I was plastered, that I'd said yes and I just couldn't remember. But I was too ashamed to argue.'

The glass toppled from Flynn's hand, rolling across the rug and leaving Scotch in its wake. Flynn watched it go, a solitary focus in a world that was shifting around him, spinning until he didn't know which way was up any more.

Maybe you didn't even know who the father was. He'd said that and she'd winced. Because she hadn't known. Because two men had taken that away from her. Had taken everything. And now she sat here relating the story in a perfectly matter-of-fact voice, as if she were putting herself apart from the memory so it couldn't hurt her any more.

He wanted to reach out to her, to touch her, to tell her he was listening now, but what right did he have? And what good would it do when she was leaving him anyway?

'I knew there was a chance I wouldn't have been able to look at my daughter without remembering that night, without reliving it.'

'And that's why you thought you couldn't love your own child.' The words rasped in his dry throat and Flynn grasped tight on to the arms of his chair to try and stop his world from tilting so far it tipped him off.

'After that day, I wasn't sure I'd ever be able to love anyone or anything again,' Helena said, and when her gaze flashed up to meet his Flynn felt it all the way deep in his soul. 'But I did. I fell in love with you, even when it was the craziest, riskiest thing I could do. And it still wasn't enough.'

Flynn swallowed, unable to find the words to respond. Helena drained the last of her whisky and put the glass next to a stack of paper on the desk before getting to her feet.

'I gave up my child, did everything our parents wanted, and it still wasn't enough for them. Eight years later, I married you to try and make up for my past mistakes and *that* wasn't enough either. So, you know what? I'm done trying to be enough for anyone else. I'm good enough for me. I'm not a monster, whatever you think.'

'Helena—I didn't—' Flynn started, but she held up a hand to stop him.

'No. You're not talking. You're listening, and then I'm leaving.' She swallowed and he could see the tears forming in her eyes. Fine. She wanted him to listen? He'd listen. And maybe some of this crazy mess would start to make sense to him at last.

'I was a child, and I was taken advantage of,' Helena went on. 'I did the best I could then, and

I'm doing the best I can now. And if that's not enough for you? It's your loss, Flynn. Because I didn't want you as a CEO or as an heir. I wasn't going to push you aside because I found a better option. I just wanted you. I wanted the future you painted for me in your wedding speech. You talked about how you can't plan for love or schedule romance—and then you went and tried to do just that. But I didn't want some spreadsheet setting out when we had sex, or had kids, or when you should buy me flowers. I wanted a real marriage—love. And that's so much more than anyone else has ever offered you.'

I just wanted you.

The words echoed in his brain until he could hear nothing else. Grasping at the arms of his chair, he tried to push himself up, to reach her, reason with her. 'Helena. I...'

'No.' She shook her head, blonde waves flying, and he knew again that he loved her. He'd used her lies and the adoption as an excuse to push her away before she could hurt or leave him. When all along she'd offered him everything he'd ever wanted—and never believed he'd deserve. 'I can't...' She bit back a sob and Flynn felt like the worst man who had ever lived. 'Look, read this. Then we can talk.' She thrust the stack of papers from his desk into his hands and he stared at it, confused.

By the time he realised what he held, the door had swung closed and she was gone.

He wanted to follow, wanted to fix things, but he didn't know where to start. And Helena had just given him the best clue he was likely to get.

Their marriage contract, except now it was covered in Helena's handwriting. The same loopy scrawl he'd seen on the back of that invitation on their wedding day, promising they would figure everything out once they were married.

Well, now that time was here.

Pouring himself another whisky, Flynn settled down to read and hoped against hope Helena's words would tell him how to make this right.

It was five days before the doctors finally agreed with Thomas's protestations that he was ready to go home.

Ever since he woke up the first day he'd been demanding to be let out, but Isabella kept telling him, 'I almost lost you, Thomas! So you are staying here until the doctors say it is time to go home.' The tone in which she said this ranged from calming to almost hysterical, depending on how belligerent he was being that day.

Helena had stayed back, letting her mother-in-law deal with him, knowing that she was the only woman he'd listen to anyway. But she'd visited every day and even managed some short civil conversations with her father. Thea's first visit had elicited rapid beeping on Thomas's heart monitor as he'd berated her, but Thea had taken everything he'd thrown at her without losing any of the serene calm she'd come to possess since running away with Zeke.

Then she'd told him in no uncertain terms that she was happy, living her life the way she wanted to, and anyway, had Isabella told Ezekiel she'd left him yet or were they waiting for him to guess?

That shut him up for almost half an hour.

But once they were all back living in the Morrison house again, it was harder to ignore the fact that Helena was there and Flynn wasn't. Or that Isabella wasn't leaving and no one had spoken to Ezekiel. Helena knew that sooner or later this all had to blow up in their faces, but she was happy to ignore the fact for as long as possible.

Until, in fact, Isabella decided she wanted to throw a party.

'It can be a welcome home party for Thomas, to celebrate his...well...'

'Survival?' Zeke suggested when his mother trailed off. 'Continued health? Heart attack?'

'His life,' Isabella said firmly. 'We could make it an engagement party for you and Thea too, perhaps,' she added with a sideways look at them.

Thea and Zeke exchanged a glance that only

lasted a moment, but appeared to convey a whole conversation.

'Actually,' Zeke said, 'it's a bit late for that.'

'A bit…late?' Isabella's eyebrows rose.

'After we left Italy…we took a flight to Vegas,' Thea explained, and Helena clapped a hand to her mouth to hold in a whoop of laughter.

'*Las* Vegas,' Isabella said for clarification, in the tone that Helena imagined she'd probably use to say 'a *brothel*'.

'Please tell me you were married by an Elvis impersonator!' Helena thumped her brother-in-law on the arm. 'And I can't believe you didn't tell me immediately!'

'She nixed the idea of Elvis, unfortunately,' Zeke said. 'But yes, we got married.'

'Well.' Isabella appeared at a loss for words, which Helena thought might be a first. It also didn't last very long. 'In that case, we'll have to make it a rather larger affair. We'll have it out at the estate, rather than here in town. I'll go and call the planner right now.' She started to head for the door, then paused and turned back to face the three of them. 'I know I…well, I might not have always showed this, but I think you did the right thing. All of you. Sometimes love is bigger than propriety and gossip. And sometimes you don't know how long you have… Anyway, I would like to celebrate the marriages of my sons.'

Thea stepped up and kissed Isabella on the cheek. 'Thank you. That means a lot.'

'When are you going to tell Dad you're leaving?' Zeke asked.

Isabella gave him a sad smile. 'If he hasn't noticed that I've gone by now, he probably never will. But yes, I have a meeting with him and my solicitor tomorrow. We'll keep everything civil and low-key. We all owe each other that much.'

It was hard to imagine, Helena thought, after all these years, that Isabella would officially step into the role and life she'd been living secretly for so long. Maybe it was a good thing, maybe not—but she wouldn't wish her father on anyone else so maybe it was just inevitable.

Isabella had always loved Thomas more than her sons, or his daughters. But until now she'd valued her social standing and reputation more than love. That shift alone…could it be the making of a new Isabella?

'Helena,' Isabella said, breaking her out of her musings. 'You did the right thing too. It might not feel like it yet, but I believe that it will.'

Helena tried to smile but the sadness within her wouldn't let her. Flynn hadn't called in the days since she'd left him in the library of what was supposed to be their home. The truth hadn't made a difference in the end. So even if marrying Flynn *had* been the right thing, for him it was still outweighed by all the wrong things she'd done before.

And no fancy party was going to change that.

'Your mother has left me.' Ezekiel entered Flynn's office without knocking and dropped into the visitor's chair. 'I just met with her and a divorce solicitor.'

Flynn wondered if this was really news to his father, whether he'd honestly thought that Isabella would come back once Thomas had recovered. 'I'm...sorry?'

Ezekiel waved a hand to dismiss Flynn's apology, as if the dissolution of his marriage was nothing but a mere inconvenience. 'It shouldn't affect things here. Thomas and I have been business partners too long to let something like this tear down everything we worked so hard to build up.'

Of course that was his concern. Business before everything else, just the same as always.

'I'm glad things will be...amicable.' What else could he say?

'In fact, she's throwing a party this weekend. You should have an invite somewhere in there.' He pointed to Flynn's in-tray. 'Celebrating your brother's quickie wedding in some Vegas casino, apparently.'

Flynn smiled as he flicked through the stack

of papers. Of course Zeke and Thea had got married, and as irreverently as possible. Finding the envelope, he ripped it open and read the invitation.

Isabella and Thomas invite you to celebrate life and love with them.

They certainly weren't wasting any time at all. And apparently his mother had given up worrying what other people thought. He approved, he thought.

Even more, he approved of this party—because Helena would be there. He'd done as she asked. He'd listened, he'd thought and he'd spent a lot of time considering her manifesto.

His mother's party would be the perfect time to show her how well he'd learned, and listened. And to tell her his new plan for their future.

As Ezekiel ambled back out of the office, Henry rapped on the door.

'You got a moment?' Henry asked.

'Of course.' Flynn gestured to the seat across the desk. 'What's up?'

Henry sat, holding a brown file tightly between two hands. 'I have the information you asked me to find. Are you sure you still want it?'

Flynn's chest tightened. 'I'm sure,' he said,

even though he wasn't. 'Thank you for doing this for me.'

Henry shrugged as he handed the file across. 'I'm just grateful you decided to look up your birth mother, rather than asking me to find the monsters who hurt Helena. After that first phone call…let's just say I had visions of having to defend you in court if you'd found them.'

'I'm trying to look to the future, not the past. And, you know, not get arrested.' Flynn held the file lightly between his fingers but didn't open it. Did he really want to know? And did it matter? Was it enough to just acknowledge that perhaps his real mother had reason to believe that he would have a better life without her, whatever happened next?

'If you want me to make contact, I can,' Henry said, nodding at the file. 'When you're ready.'

'Maybe.' He'd thought this was what he needed, to prove to Helena that he'd moved on. But the more he'd studied her manifesto, the more he'd realised this wasn't about adoption—his, or her daughter's. It was about them finally allowing themselves to be happy.

He opened his bottom desk drawer and slipped the file inside. 'Not just yet,' he said. 'But soon, I think.'

'Okay.' Henry shrugged. 'Anything you want me to do in the meantime?'

Flynn smiled. 'How would you like to come out to the family estate for a party this weekend?'

'Sounds good,' Henry said. 'What's the catch?'

'I need you to go and pick something up for me first. From Italy.'

CHAPTER THIRTEEN

'YOU LOOK BEAUTIFUL.' Thea finished zipping up Helena's deep blue cocktail dress and stepped back. 'Flynn won't know what's hit him.'

'Zeke, last I saw,' Helena joked. She didn't know how much Zeke had told Thea about their visit to Flynn, but she'd seen Thea cooing over his bruised hand afterwards.

Thea sat on the bed, smoothing out her own bright red dress. Isabella had wanted her to wear white, but Thea had been adamant that she had already done the wedding thing. Almost twice.

'Are you going to be okay down there tonight? With him here, I mean?' Thea asked.

Helena shrugged. 'I don't think it matters if I am or not. Even if he wasn't my husband, he would still be Zeke's brother, Isabella's son. He's going to be around, always. I'm going to have to get used to it some time or another.' Not to mention the fact that she'd met with Isabella's divorce solicitor the day before. At some point, she'd have to sit across a table from Flynn and discuss what happened next. She wasn't looking forward to it but if Isabella could do it, so could she.

Thea checked her watch. 'It's time. The first guests are probably already arriving.'

Zeke met them at the top of the stairs and they headed down together. It was strange, Helena thought. It had been so many years since the four of them had been at a party together in this house. So very much had changed in the years since Zeke had left home but, in lots of ways, it felt like just another party.

At least she was old enough to drink at them these days.

'There you all are!' Isabella called from the hallway. 'Come get a glass of bubbly and say hello to some people.' Helena and Thea exchanged a glance, grabbed champagne flutes and headed in.

The party was in full swing by the time she caught her first glimpse of Flynn. Isabella had collared him by the door and was holding his arm tightly as she spoke close to his ear. Helena had no idea what she was saying but she suspected she didn't want to hang around and find out, either.

With so many people in attendance, it wasn't too hard to keep moving between the crowd and stay out of Flynn's way. It was entirely possible he was doing the same thing, of course. She was under no illusion that he'd be desperate to talk to her, either. If he had been, if he'd moved past his anger and disgust, he would have called by now.

People would talk, of course, if they weren't seen together tonight—but people would talk anyway, the moment the divorce was announced. Maybe it was better to get the rumours started now so it wouldn't be so shocking later. They could even bury the news under the announcement of Thea and Zeke's wedding.

Helena looked around for Thea and her husband. This was their night, after all—theirs and Isabella's and Thomas's. She'd celebrate with them and then she'd disappear upstairs for an early night when no one would notice. Thea could tell people she had a headache if anyone asked.

There. She had a plan. Flynn would be so proud.

The minutes ticked by unbearably slowly, but eventually Helena figured it had to be safe to escape. She was halfway across the room to let Thea know she was going when she heard the sound of metal on glass.

'Ladies and gentlemen, if I could ask for your attention, please?' Flynn's voice rang out across the party and stopped Helena in her tracks. 'My mother has asked me to say a few words.'

Of course she had. Of course Isabella would be behind this.

And of course she'd be grabbing hold of Helena's arm right now.

'Come on,' she said as she dragged her closer to where Flynn was making his speech. 'I don't want to miss this.'

I do, though! Helena sighed and allowed herself to be dragged. But after this she was going to bed.

'As you probably all know, my mother and Thomas asked us here tonight to celebrate life and love, in its many and wondrous forms. We are all, as I know you are, giving thanks for Thomas's swift recovery and hoping for plenty more life for him to enjoy yet. And we're celebrating a marriage—yes, another one!' A smatter of laughter at that, and Helena felt too many eyes on her.

Not Flynn's, though. He hadn't even glanced in her direction.

'Thea and Zeke's wasn't a conventional wedding, by all accounts, but, since nothing else about their relationship was conventional either, it seems only right that it happened this way.' Flynn looked out over the crowd as he spoke, as if he was meeting every person's gaze individually. 'There's no point pretending you don't already know the story. Thea and I were, only last month, intending to marry each other—until Zeke drove back into our lives and reminded us all of something important. The power love has to override all plans, make a mockery of any schedule and lead us to places we never thought we'd want to go.'

Helena's heart clenched at his words, so similar to the speech he'd made on their wedding day. The tightness in her chest only grew when Flynn turned to gaze directly at her as he spoke again.

'Since my own marriage, I seem to have learnt a lot about love, and about life. Far more than I ever knew before. And that is entirely down to my beautiful wife, Helena.' He motioned towards her and Helena blushed at the 'ahh's from the crowd.

What was he doing? Keeping up the charade? Making it impossible for her to walk away? Or was it just possible that this was something else? Something more?

Helena held her breath and allowed herself a moment to hope.

'In fact, I needed so much education that my wife wrote me a memo, to help me make sense of it all.' The crowd laughed as, from a side table nearby, Flynn picked up a stack of paper and held it up. Helena's eyes widened. Her manifesto!

She'd poured every hope and dream she had into that pile of paper. Every small detail and moment that would make her future happy. And Flynn had read it, and carried it with him tonight. Did that mean…did he want them to have another chance?

'I won't read this aloud, although I think every

married couple should have a copy. In fact, I have a photocopy here for you, Zeke!' More laughter, and Helena grasped at her skirt with clammy hands. She wanted this over. She wanted to know what this was, what he was doing. She wanted to *understand*.

'But I did want to quote just a couple of lines.' He flicked through the pages to a sheet towards the end, and Helena held her breath. 'Helena wrote: "Love is about more than where it can take you or what it can provide—a marriage, a home, a family, status or money. Love is about experiencing any or all of those things with the one person who makes them worthwhile. Who makes life meaningful."'

Flynn lowered the paper and gazed out over the crowd at her again, and the hope that had budded tightly in Helena's heart began to blossom.

'Helena is the only person who could ever and will ever bring that meaning into my life, whatever our future brings. And I feel so incredibly lucky to have realised that, at last.'

He looked away, smiling out at his audience again, but Helena didn't mind. *Those* were the words she hadn't even known she needed to hear.

'Life doesn't follow a plan, any more than love does,' Flynn went on. 'Sometimes the best things in life just happen—and so do the worst things. What makes it harder is that sometimes you can't even tell which is which. But life doesn't go backwards, and neither does love. You can't switch love off or pretend it never happened. All you can do is love and live in the now, and look to the future with amazement and joy. And that, my friends, is what I wish for my brother and his wife, and for my mother and Thomas. And, most of all, for Helena and me.'

He stepped down to wild applause, but he didn't seem to hear it. Instead, he walked straight to Helena, took her hand and placed something in it, folding her fingers over it before she could see. But she knew from the shape, the feel of it, exactly what Flynn had given her.

And she smiled and let him take her other hand and lead her outside.

Flynn's heart beat double time as he walked Helena out to the outdoor seating area behind the house. There was a slight drizzle in the air, which he'd normally hate, but tonight it just meant that they were able to be alone.

'My manifesto,' Helena said. 'You know that was just a sort of joke, really.'

'No, it wasn't,' Flynn said, and tried not to focus on how long it had been since he'd seen her, and how much he had hurt her. 'It told me everything you felt and wanted. It let me know you, see you clearer than I ever had. That and finally hearing the full story about what happened to you.'

She looked away and Flynn reached out to rest his palm against her cheek, to keep her eyes on him. 'Why didn't you tell me in Tuscany?'

'Because it wouldn't have made any difference,' Helena said, and her mouth twisted up into an almost smile. 'Everything you said was still true.'

'No,' Flynn said, as firmly as he could. He had to make her believe this. 'I judged you as the person I thought you were, without even thinking about you as the woman I'd fallen in love with. I…before I read what you'd written, I was angry with myself for falling in love with you. For loving someone who had done something I considered unforgivable. But now…now I feel I know you better. And I know, even if you don't, that the woman who wrote this doesn't have it in her not to love. You think you wouldn't have loved that child? You're wrong.'

'In which case, I still did the wrong thing by giving her away.' Helena pulled away. 'So nothing changes.'

'I changed,' Flynn said quietly. 'You changed me. I thought…I thought I had to follow a plan, my rules, my schedule. That anything outside of them was wrong. By my rules, what you did was wrong, yes. But you don't live by my rules—or anyone else's. You made the decision you had to make at the time, with the best information you had. And that decision had a big part in shaping who you are today, in making you the woman I love.'

'So...you're saying you forgive me?' Helena chewed on her lower lip as she looked up at him with those big bluebell eyes.

'I'm saying that you don't need my forgiveness. You need to forgive yourself.'

She couldn't stop the tears, didn't even want to. And, as Flynn pulled her into his arms and held her against his chest, she knew she'd come home again, at last.

'Do you forgive me?' Flynn asked against her hair. 'The things I said...they were unforgivable, I know. But do you think...?'

'Yes,' Helena said. 'I forgive you.' But if forgiveness was the start for them, she knew it wouldn't be everything. They had a long way to go yet.

'But, Flynn,' she said, leaning back to see his face, 'I can't just forget—any of it. You, or what happened to me. That's going to take time.'

'I have all the time in the world for you.' Flynn set his cheek against her hair and Helena sighed. It felt right. She wanted it to be right. And yet...

'I can't promise you anything,' she said. 'Well,

nothing beyond the fact that I'm apparently always going to love you. Can't seem to shake that one.'

'Good.'

'But I don't know if I'll ever be ready to have children.' It hurt to say the words, hurt to think it. She'd been happy, imagining her life without kids, until she'd married Flynn. Now, it stung—not just because she couldn't give him what she knew he wanted, but because for the first time she wondered if she might want it too.

Flynn loosened his arms from around her waist and took her hands in his instead, rubbing his thumb over the knuckles of the fingers, still wrapped around the object he'd placed in her palm.

'I promise you this,' he said, his expression solemn. 'There is no schedule for our life together, no plan. Not any more. If it happens one day that you turn to me and tell me you're ready to try for a baby, I'll be the happiest man on earth. And if it doesn't?' He shrugged. 'I'll still be the happiest man on earth because I'll be married to you.'

Slowly, he dropped to his knees and Helena bit back a sob. Could he really be giving her everything she'd ever wanted? And could she forgive herself enough to accept?

Peeling back her fingers, he took her engagement ring from her hand and placed it at the tip of her ring finger. 'Helena Juliette Ashton. Will you do me the honour of being my wife?'

Through her tears, Helena giggled. 'Isn't this where we came in?' she asked as he slid the ring home.

'It's the only place I want to be,' Flynn said, and tugged her down for a kiss.

EPILOGUE

THE TUSCAN SUN shone down as bright as ever, and Helena pulled the brim of her straw hat down to shade her eyes as she watched her niece and nephew chase each other through the grapevines, racing after their new friend Casper.

It had been five years since she and Flynn had first visited Gia's vineyard, but Helena still felt exactly the same sense of home as she had the first time.

Up ahead, Thea and Zeke quizzed Gia about her growing methods, about how the wine was made, and Gia answered patiently the questions she must have been asked a thousand times before.

Helena tuned them out and focused instead on the warm sun on her shoulders, the buzz of summer insects in the air, and her husband's hand in her own.

'This is a wonderful place for a family, don't you think?' she asked, and Flynn murmured his agreement.

'I'm so glad we got to bring Thea and the kids here,' she went on. 'It's good to share this place with them.'

'It's been a great holiday,' Flynn agreed, but Helena knew he was barely listening—too languid and lazy in the sun.

'Maybe we'll come back again next year with our own child,' she said as casually as she could.

Flynn stopped walking and Helena grinned, ducking her head so he couldn't see.

'Helena. Are you saying…? Do you think you might be ready to maybe…?' It wasn't often Flynn fell over his words. It was kind of nice to hear.

She beamed up at him, loving the amazed wonder on his face. 'I'm saying it's a little late for that conversation.'

His eyes widened further. 'You mean you're already…? And you're okay? Do you want to talk about it?'

'I'm fine,' Helena assured him, taking his hand and placing it on her still flat stomach. 'We're fine.'

'We said we'd talk about this if you ever changed your mind. I don't want you to feel—'

'All I feel is happy—' Helena interrupted '—happy and grateful and loved.'

Flynn let out a long breath. 'You're sure?'

'I'm sure.' She grinned. 'And you did say you wanted to be more spontaneous.'

'I couldn't have planned this any better,' Flynn said, and kissed her.

* * * * *

LARGER-PRINT BOOKS!

GET 2 FREE LARGER-PRINT NOVELS PLUS
2 FREE GIFTS!

HARLEQUIN

Romance

From the Heart, For the Heart

SPECIAL EXCERPT FROM

HARLEQUIN®

Romance

*Read on for a sneak preview of Jessica Gilmore's
exciting new title,*

THE HEIRESS'S SECRET BABY

RESOLUTELY POLLY HELD the glass up over the man's face
and tipped it. For one long moment she held it still so that the
water was perfectly balanced right at the rim, clear drops so
very close to spilling over the thin edge.

And then she allowed her hand to move the glass over the
tipping point, a perfect stream of cold water falling like rain
onto the peacefully slumbering face below.

Polly didn't quite know what to expect; anger, shock,
contrition or even no reaction at all. He was so very deeply
asleep after all. But what she didn't expect was for one red-
rimmed eye to lazily open, for a smile to play around the
disturbingly well-cut mouth or for a hand to shoot out and
grab her wrist.

Caught by surprise, she stumbled forward, falling against
the chaise as the hand snuck around her waist, pulling her
down, pulling her close.

"Bonjour, chérie." His voice was low, gravelly with
sleep and deeply, unmistakably French. "If you wanted me
to wake up you only had to ask."

It was the shock, that was all. Otherwise she would have
moved, called for help, disentangled herself from the strong
arm anchoring her firmly against the bare chest. And she
would never, *ever* have allowed his other hand to slip around

her neck in an oddly sweet caress while he angled his mouth toward hers—she would have moved away long before the hard mouth claimed hers in a distinctly unsleepy way.

It was definitely the shock keeping her paralyzed under his touch—and she was definitely *not* leaning into the kiss, opening herself up to the pressure of his mouth on hers, the touch of his hand moving up her back, slipping round her rib cage, brushing against the swell of her breast.

Hang on, his hand was where?

Polly pulled away, jumping up off the chaise, resisting the urge to scrub the kiss off her tingling mouth.

Or to lean back down and let him claim her again.

"What do you think you're doing?"

"Saying *au revoir* of course." He had shifted position and was leaning against the back of the chaise, his eyes skimming every inch of her until she wanted to wrap her arms around her torso, shielding herself from his insolent gaze.

"*Au revoir?*" Was she going mad? Where were the panicked apologies and the scuttling out of her office?

"Of course." He raised an eyebrow. "As you are dressed to leave I thought you were saying goodbye. But if it was more of a good morning—" the smile widened "—even better."

"I am not saying *au revoir* or good morning or anything but *what on earth are you doing in my office and where are your clothes?*"

*Don't miss this sparkling new romance
by Jessica Gilmore, THE HEIRESS'S SECRET BABY!*

*Available February 2015 wherever Harlequin®
Romance books and ebooks are sold!*

www.Harlequin.com

HREXP0115